Paris Forever

LYNN JOSEPH

BLACK MERMAID PRESS
BOOKS THAT CHALLENGE THE STATUS QUO

Interior art by Annalize McLean, PhD

 Created with Vellum

Get a Free Romance Novel!

Escape to Italy with Princess Abroad, a captivating royal romance filled with love, adventure, and breathtaking scenery. Sign up for my newsletter today and claim your free copy!

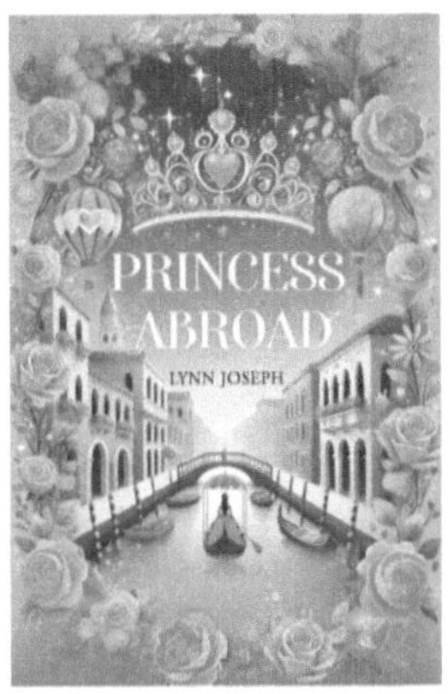

Sign up here —> https://BookHip.com/NKSQGRS

Author's Note

Paris Forever is Book 4 of the Walker Sisters Forever series. Each book is a standalone, but they are interconnected. Just to get you caught up, Daisy and Leo met in *Sangria Forever*, Book 3, in Porto, Portugal, when Daisy went to visit her sister Corinne, who was studying in Porto.

Paris Forever is about Daisy and Leo finding each other again after a long separation.

My goal is to be as authentic as possible in writing each of these travel abroad romances. I visited Paris twice and researched what Daisy's life would be like there.

I also researched Leo's best friend, James's culture, and tried to portray him accurately. I am sure I missed a lot. My sincere apologies for any inaccuracies, which are all my fault and unintended.

I am happy you are joining me on these journeys of traveling and falling in love.

Thank you,

Lynn Joseph

Life is a flower, of which love is the honey.
Victor Hugo

For those who believe in fairy tales and happy ever after!

Chapter One

DAISY

"Real girls don't get fairy tales, Daisy. Grow up. I'm younger than you, and even I know better."

I stare at my laptop screen with its sparkling photos of beautiful Paris and try to block out Emerald's annoying voice.

Ms. Know-it-all who already had two boyfriends before receiving her acceptance letter to the University of Hawaii. A thorn in my side doesn't begin to describe my youngest sister.

"I don't believe that," I mutter. But not loud enough that she can hear me.

As the hype girl for my four sisters, I'm used to being the wallflower.

But now, at nineteen, a sophomore in college with the chance to spend one year abroad in the most beautiful city in the world, things will change for me.

I know it.

"I'm going to Paris," I tell Emerald. "Anything can happen there. Even fairy tales."

She scoffs, "I don't want you to get your feelings hurt, is all."

Yeah, right.

Of my four sisters, Emerald is the only one I don't get along well with.

Let's say she makes my life difficult by being born one year after me and then screaming louder than me to keep the attention on herself.

Not to mention, she's so sure of herself all the time.

So unlike me. I'm constantly second-guessing myself. I dream up stories to fill in the lack of real-life experiences.

If any of the Walker sisters will win a Nobel Prize, host her own podcast, or run for President, it won't be me.

But this is not a story about my sisters.

It's not about Ava, my oldest sister, who traveled to Italy and fell in love while learning to make award-winning gelato.

Or Bridget, who is so talented that she runs a theater in Greece and found her true love there.

Or gorgeous, multi-lingual Corrine with her handsome fiancé, a European footballer in Portugal.

And it's not about Emerald, who stole Jackson Banza from me when I was a senior in high school and she was a junior.

She dated the handsome jock I'd been in love with from afar for only a few months, then decided she needed space.

So, yeah. This story is *not* about any of my dynamic, over-achieving, gorgeous sisters whom I love with all my heart. Even if I don't see eye to eye with all of them.

This is *my* story.

Daisy Walker.

Quiet, shy, face-stuck-in-a-romance book, queen of "never say never, *it could happen to me*" sister.

So what if I've never had a boyfriend, or even been kissed. And maybe I lied a tiny bit by telling everyone I kissed the handsome Leo whom I met in Portugal when I visited Corrine.

It was all in my imagination. But it seemed so real it might as well have happened.

THE SAND IS COOL BENEATH MY FEET AS I STAND WITH Leo near the edge of the beach, the reggae music pulsing through the air, blending with the sound of the waves rolling in.

The stage lights cast a warm glow over the crowd, catching bits of seashells in the sand, making everything shimmer.

Leo leans back, his blond hair wind-tousled, eyes half-closed, nodding along to the beat. He looks so relaxed, so alive, like he was made for this exact moment.

"Do you always listen to reggae?" he asks, glancing down at me, a hint of a smile in those impossibly blue eyes.

I shrug, feeling a little shy, but the music gives me courage. "Not always, but I like it. It's . . . freeing."

He grins, eyes twinkling, and I can't help but smile back, feeling my cheeks warm.

"Freeing," he echoes as if he's trying out the word, letting it settle between us. "The only time I feel totally free is when I'm surfing. Riding on top of the waves, not knowing what's coming next."

I imagine him on his board, all blond hair and ease, riding waves like he's part of them, like he belongs there. "Must be nice to have something like that," I say softly, half to myself. "To feel that . . . free."

He tilts his head, his gaze turning serious. "I don't always feel that way. Most of the time, I don't have a choice about my life. It's all planned out." He gives a wistful sigh. "What about you?"

I shake my head. "I have a lot of choices. Where to go to college, where to live or travel, or what I want to do. I feel free in that sense. Nothing is expected, which makes it easy."

"That's wonderful, Daisy. It's not like that for me."

"Well, maybe that's why we met," I tease. "For me to help you feel a little freer."

He laughs. "That would be perfect."

I look away, focusing on the waves, the rhythm of the ocean. But he reaches out, tucks a loose curl behind my ear, his fingers lingering a second longer than they need to.

"You've got a good heart, Daisy," he says, his voice low. "You don't need to change a thing. Just . . . don't hide it, okay?"

Something swells in my chest, something warm and new. I nod, biting my lip to keep from smiling too wide. He pulls me into a hug, and I let myself sink into his warmth, feeling his heartbeat against mine, steady and real.

For the rest of the concert, we stand there, side by side, his arm around me, like it's the most natural thing in the world.

I don't know if it's the music or the way he looks at me, but in that moment with Leo, I feel freer than I've ever felt.

Like I didn't have to worry about what's coming next.

I shake my head to clear away the memory of how it felt to be around him—his energy was like the sea. Exciting, unpredictable, but yet, somehow soothing at the same time.

The way he stared into my eyes made me feel . . . *precious*. As if I mattered to him.

In the short time we'd spent together, I felt seen for the first time by a boy.

I stopped questioning my weight, my chubby cheeks and my dimpled thighs. I was lush and lovely and perfect with him.

Chapter Two

DAISY

Convincing Dad that I should go alone to Paris for one year isn't easy.

We're in the kitchen of our home in Portland, Maine. I've dreaded this conversation, so I made his favorite cookies and his favorite Dole pineapple punch that I whipped up in the blender.

He saw right thought it. "What's this about, Daisy?"

I hand him the acceptance letter to the Sorbonne University, Paris's premier college, and the packet of information.

"Wow! This is impressive, Daisy. Congratulations. But *why*?" Emotions race across his face. "Why are you leaving me too?"

"Daddy, it's an amazing opportunity." I lean my head on his shoulder. "I'll be walking in the footsteps of great writers, like Richard Wright, Ernest Hemingway, F. Scott Fitzgerald, and your favorite, James Baldwin."

Ava, my oldest and favorite sister, is there to back me up.

"You love James Baldwin, Daddy," Ava reminds him. "Daisy

wants to be a writer. Where better for her to learn and be inspired than the city that inspired the greats?"

Daddy gazes from Ava to me. "I'm being ambushed, here. There's lots of great writers in New England to be inspired by."

He's almost pouting. "You girls go traveling, then you fall in love and don't come back." He leans against the kitchen counter, looking so sad I felt terrible to be the cause of wiping the smile off his brown face.

"Oh, Daddy. I'll be back. It's just one year. And I promise not to fall in love."

I say that last part with my fingers crossed behind my back.

"That's what Bridget and Corrine said, too."

I can't bear how sad his face looks.

"I don't have to go." My heart clenches at the idea of giving up Paris.

"No," he waves away my offer. "You must go."

"Of course, Daisy has to go to Paris," Ava says, matter-of-factly. "Don't forget I'm here."

I sigh with relief. "Right. You have Ava. *She* came back home from Italy."

Ava winks at me. "Besides, Daisy must see Leo again. We can't deny her a romance."

"What?" I sputter. "That's not why I'm going to Paris. Leo's not even going to be there. He's in South Africa surfing." A fact I know from stalking his Instagram page.

"I think," I add quickly at Ava's raised eyebrows.

I don't say aloud that he wouldn't date me even if he were in Paris.

I've seen the women hanging around him in photos. I'm nothing like the petite, bikini-clad surfer girls with their beachy tans and sun-streaked hair blowing in the tropical breezes.

I prefer romantic florals and lace. Big floppy hats in the sun. And no one could accuse me of being a tiny thing.

And I'm definitely not like the French girls with their all-black clothing, a color I would never wear, not even as an accessory.

I may be heading to Paris for many reasons, but to date Leo is not one of them. At least that's what I tell myself.

"He's my friend," I say to Dad and Ava. "That's all."

I bite my bottom lip to stop saying more. Friends would be a stretch from a person who hasn't texted me back in months.

One day we're laughing, chatting, sharing our lives one text message at a time. The next, he's gone radio silent.

I get that he's busy with his gap year of traveling and surfing, but to just disappear out of my life like that. It was so heartbreaking that I decided to confide in Corrine. After all, she introduced us.

At first, she said what I was thinking, "That doesn't seem like Leo."

A few days later she called and said, "Forget him, Daisy. Move on. Some people come into our lives for a season, not a lifetime."

I asked what she was talking about. She repeated her cryptic message and added another, "He's part of your journey, sis, but he's not your destination."

I was like, "Huh?" But that was all she had to say.

Since then, which was two months ago, I've cried in silence whenever I look at his photos. For me, Leo was both my journey *and* my destination.

We're still social media friends. We still follow each other, although I try my best not to Like or comment on his photos.

If I could only understand why he stopped talking to me.

Did he meet someone else?

Did he forget the chubby girl in Portugal whose heart lit up whenever he was around?

Did he forget Paris? He introduced me to Paris. It was a short hop from Porto, Portugal, but a whole different world. Instead of beaches, we had boulevards. Instead of codfish cakes, we had crêpes.

My heart twists at the memory of one night with Leo, just us and a Grand Marnier crêpe set on fire between us in a tiny Parisian crêperie.

He grinned as the flames danced, and we laughed, pretending to catch them on our forks.

Each bite was warm and sweet, the orange liqueur lingering, but it wasn't the taste I remembered. It was the way he looked at me between bites, his ice blue eyes melting with the flames. All soft and full, like he was already memorizing me.

For a moment, the whole world seemed as small as our table tucked away in the corner of that shop.

Chapter Three

LEO

The phone buzzes next to my bed. I slap a hand down to shut it up, but it keeps on buzzing like a busy little bee.

"What?" I ask crankily, putting the phone to my ear.

The screen shows it's only 3:30 a.m. We arrived back at the beach cottage hours ago, but I feel sluggish from the whiskey and wine still rolling in my veins.

It was someone's birthday. Another reason to drink, be merry, and forget the real world.

"It's the middle of the night," I snap into my phone.

"Excuse me, Your Royal Highness."

"Olivia?" I jump up. Why is our Chief of Staff calling me?

"The Queen wishes to speak to you."

My blood curdles. "At 3:30 a.m.?"

I pull on a shirt and wrap my body in the blanket. It feels wrong to talk to my mother in an undressed state. Even though it's not a video call.

"Hi, Mother," I say.

"Hello, Leopold. I'm sorry to call you at this hour."

I inhale sharply. "What's wrong?" My mother's voice is wobbly. She is fiercely strong and adamant about protocol. Wobbly is not in her DNA.

Plus, we have an established time to call once per week.

"Your father needs you to come home."

"What? Why? Is he okay?"

I can't imagine a universe where my impervious father admits that he needs anything. Much less me.

When she doesn't answer, my heart triples its beat. "Mother?"

"I'm sorry, son. I know you have another month of freedom, as you call it, but he needs you. I held off as long as I could."

I swallow hard. "Of course, I will come home. What's wrong with Father?"

I hold my breath, waiting for her answer. *Please don't let it have come back*. I pray hard.

"It came back," her voice cracks. Soft sobs start from the other end of the phone.

A barrel of curse words rolls through my brain. I manage to stop them from exiting my mouth.

"I'm so sorry to hear that, Mother. I'll be there tomorrow."

"Olivia will arrange it," she says, tears heavy in her voice.

"Have you told Leif?"

"He's at University."

I swallow. I hear her unspoken words, "*Where you should be, too.*"

"What did the doctor say?" I change the subject.

"One year. If we're lucky."

"We're lucky, mother."

"One year is nothing," she says. "I'm not ready to lose our King."

"Me either," I say softly. "None of us are."

After hanging up, I sit on the edge of my bed, head in my hands. The last thing I can do now is go back to sleep.

"Damn!" I kick the blanket on the floor. Poor Dad. Just last year he was beating me at polo. He was back to his old self.

He was arguing with the ministers, dancing with Mother in the gardens, his favorite part of the castle, and he gave me this year off because he wanted me to live fully before I had to take over.

I pray silently. Bargaining for Dad's health. He was too young, too needed, too special to die. Although none of those things ever stopped death.

Now, my destiny was calling me.

At least I'd had my year of travels. When I arrived in South Africa, my best friend, James Langa Zulu joined me for a month of surfing. As the future King of the Zulu Nation, he had the same life path as I did.

Two princes whose destinies had been set from birth. Surfing was our way of rebelling a little from a life of duty, honor, and expectations.

The morning light slowly seeps through my bedroom window illuminating the grey waves outside. I watch the sky change from dark blue to glowing pink.

It reminds me of Daisy Walker's love for pink flowers. *Everything* reminds me of her.

I don't know if it's because I'm sad about my father's illness or worried about my future, but a strange feeling floods my entire being, starting in my heart.

I, Leopold Olef Victor Montclair, Crown Prince of Arandel, am in love with Daisy Belinda Walker of Portland, Maine.

Despite the tragic circumstances that have forced this revelation, I know it's true.

And there is nothing I can do about it right now. Maybe ever.

I lean against the window and press my face to the glass. The ocean is a constant. A massive barrier between me and Daisy.

My brother says I have a history of avoiding things I don't want to handle.

Like university and taking a gap year before getting ready to be king.

And ghosting Daisy because our relationship can't go anywhere.

Yup, that is high on the list of things I am avoiding.

The truth is, she thinks I'm Leo from Austria. She doesn't know I'm Crown Prince Leopold of Arandel. I lied to her, to her sister, to everyone so I could have my freedom to travel.

How can I be worthy of Daisy after that?

Chapter Four

LEO

The sun glints off the breaking waves like it wants me to see all I'm leaving. I stuff my wet suits into my suitcase before I realize I won't need any surf gear where I'm going.

"Dude, what's going on?" James appears in the doorway, rubbing his eyes.

I fill him in quickly about my father's returning cancer. The one-year prognosis.

He curses loudly. He grabs his suitcase and starts throwing random clothes into it.

"What are you doing?"

"I'm going with you, duh."

"What about the surf competition coming up? You've been practicing and training hard."

"So have you."

"But I must go. You don't have to."

"I have to. I'm your best friend. And you'll need me at your coronation, no? Wait. Are you crying, dude?"

I shake my head. "Montclairs don't cry."

"Right, you're inhuman."

"Something like that."

"When does the royal jet arrive? Or should we take mine?"

"It's already at the airport. Olivia sent it before I even got Mom's call. Olivia doesn't play around."

"Ohh! Who is *Olivia?*"

I smack my friend on his back. "She's twice your age. And I need her to help me run the country, so don't even think about flirting with her."

"Even better. A forbidden romance."

I groan. "Did you hear the part about my needing her?"

James stops swinging his arms in circles. "Is your father really dying?"

I stop throwing clothes in suitcases. I swallow hard.

"Yes, he is."

"It's why I'm going with you, bro," he says softly.

My head tilts. I get a closer look at the sincerity in his eyes.

"I thought it was for my coronation?"

He sucks his teeth. "You've seen one crown, you've seen them all."

He pulls on sweatpants and a jersey. Slaps a Billabong cap on his head and smiles. "How do I look?"

"You've looked better," I say honestly. "But I'll give you a thumbs up for speed."

"Well, you look awful. No thumbs up for you."

"That's life."

"It bites."

I laugh at James's comeback.

I'm grateful he's coming with me. His company always keeps my spirits up. I need it more than ever now.

"Hey, King Leo, can I like . . . be your man-in-waiting?"

I snort. "No."

"A trusted advisor?"

"No."

"Then what? I need an official title for the Kingdom of Arandel."

"You've got your title. Prince James Langa of the Zulu Nation. What more do you need? By the way, did you tell your father you're leaving with me?"

He shrugs. "No. But we princes must stick together. He'll understand. I'll tell him it's for future diplomatic relations."

I smile tightly. "It won't be a lie."

A horn blares outside our cottage door.

"You ready? Where's your diplomatic passport?"

James runs to his room and back, breathing hard. He waves the passport in the air.

"You're already displaying your ruling powers. Imagine denying me entrance to your kingdom without my passport."

"It's Olivia who will deny you, not me."

"This Olivia gets more intriguing by the minute."

"Just get in the car." I shove James ahead of me out the door.

As we leave the beach and head along the highway to the airport, my mind wanders to Daisy. What is she doing right now? Is she on her way to Paris? Does she remember when we were in Paris together for a few days?

Probably not.

I scroll through my phone, staring at her photos. She is one of the few people I have on my private social media accounts, where I can be myself and not a royal. Everyone on my private accounts knows not to mention my status. Because they too are trying to forget their own alter egos.

My mind drifts back to the day I first met Daisy. She'd come to the café with her sister Corrine. I'd been working at the café in Porto, Portugal, to get real-life experience. My shift had ended at nine that night, and all I could think about was finding the beautiful American girl with the slanted eyes and long ringlets.

I wished I knew where her sister Corrine lived. Corrine came into the café daily to study before her classes, but we'd never really talked. How was I supposed to know she had a sister like Daisy—the most beautiful girl I'd ever seen?

After work, I wandered through the two main streets lined with bars and restaurants, hoping I'd spot her. It was where everyone went to drink, dance, and hang out with friends—locals, tourists, students—everyone. I think I went into every bar along those streets, just in case she was there. I had to see her again.

Then, the next day, I walked into the café for my shift at three, and there she was. Daisy had come back. She was sitting at the same table outside, even though the November air was chilly. I clocked in, but as soon as I saw her, I knew I couldn't stay. I switched shifts with another server so I could leave at six, and I asked her, "What are we going to do?"

When six came, we strolled together along the Douro River. My stomach was doing flips, and I couldn't get my face to stop smiling. Everything was in a rosy glow, as if someone had switched on a giant light bulb in the sky that was shining down even at dusk.

I remember touching her arm to point out the old-fashioned boats carrying barrels of wine from up the Douro Valley. I could've walked next to her, arm in arm, all night long.

It felt like such a fairy tale that at one point, she turned to me and asked, "Is this real?"

I shook my head and said, "I don't think so."

And we both laughed. Her laugh made me feel as though I'd just handed her the moon.

The question burning a hole in my chest as we headed to the airport and back to my real life is, "Will I ever see her again?"

Kingdom of Arandel

Chapter Five

DAISY

I'm in Paris!

I send that message to my sisters and my father and post it on my social media accounts, where I have mostly bookish friends who read romance novels like I do.

The taxi drops me off in front of my new home for the next year.

Standing outside and looking up, I'm shocked to see a vertical garden climbing up the exterior walls—not trailing vines or ivy, but a real garden with flowering bushes.

It's incredible.

When I was admitted to Sorbonne University, one of the most elite learning institutions in the world, I thought I'd be staying in a dorm.

Turned out I had to find my own apartment. And it wasn't easy.

I had to figure out which of the twenty Parisian neighborhoods, called arrondissements, I wanted to live in, or rather, which ones I could afford with financial aid, summer job earnings, and the college fund left to me by my mother.

I decided on the Second Arrondissement.

It is close to the Louvre and next to the historic street, Rue Montorgueil, with many 17th- and 18th-century buildings, including the famous Pâtisserie Stohrer, the oldest patisserie in Paris. I heard the pastries there will break my heart.

The apartment is a bit of a trek to my classes at the Sorbonne, but I get to walk past the Notre Dame Cathedral and the Shakespeare & Co. bookstore while strolling along the Seine River.

I'd googled the area thoroughly and couldn't wait to explore.

But I didn't expect a garden on the walls of the building.

I climb the spiral wooden staircase to the third floor with a colossal smile on my face. The stairs are ancient. I wonder who else has walked up and down them.

Jim Morrison? James Baldwin?

I stop at the third floor and look around. A sign says "2."

What? I forgot the first floor is considered ground zero in Europe. So, the third floor is actually on the *fourth* landing.

I trudge up another set of curving stairs, huffing and puffing, sweat running down my face and my heart racing a mile a minute.

Seriously?

No wonder these French people are so slim.

I stare down the middle of the curved stairs. My large suitcase sits alone down at ground zero.

There's no way I can drag that up here by myself. I hope my roommate can help. We should be able to bring it up between the two of us.

When I arrive at the third (really fourth) floor, I collapse on the top stair and grab my chest. I have not trained for this.

A loud, dry cough escapes my throat. Like a smoker hacking to death.

The door clicks open behind me, and I jump.

"You're here!" A voice booms. "And you're so pretty! Look at those swinging curls. And your bag of books tumbling out. You're a Black Belle. I'm the Beast. We're perfect."

I blink hard.

I'm not a short person, but the person in front of me is at least six feet, seven inches tall and dressed head to toe in glittery clothing. Like a giant doll.

I blink again.

"Oh, honey, I'm not *that* beastly looking."

I physically shake myself to refocus. "I'm sorry. I don't mean to be rude." I jump up and shake the giant's hand.

The glittering creature nods. "Where's the rest of your luggage?"

I point down the stairs. "I was hoping you could help me."

"Me? I don't lift a thing if I can help it. But, let's see . . . ."

At that moment, the front door to our building opens, and someone enters.

I can't see who or what is below because my roommate leans across me and purrs in French, "*Mon amour. Juste à temps.*"

I slide back down to sit on the landing, still trying to catch my breath.

I've been studying French like crazy, so I know my roommate called the new person, "My love" and then said, "Just in time."

A flurry of French flies over my head.

All I know is that my luggage is making its way up the stairs on the broad shoulders of someone taking the steps two at a time.

For real? I could barely do one.

I swear I've entered another dimension.

"Honey, come inside. Your flowers are slipping away."

"What? I mean *Quoi?*"

"Your fleurs."

When I realize that my roommate is warning me that my flowered dress is getting dirty because I'm sitting on the floor, I leap up and face my luggage carrier.

"Whoa!"

"That's what I said when I saw this beautiful man," my roommate says. "At least we agree on some things."

The hunk of a man rests my bag down gently on the landing without a single out-of-breath pant.

"*Merci*," I thank the man in French. He looks like he's my age.

"No worries," he says with an American accent. He flashes his dimples in a broad smile.

"Howdy, Ma'am," he says to my roommate.

"I adore American cowboys," my roommate gushes, "don't you?"

"And we adore the French." He tips an imaginary hat at us.

"Feel free to call me if you gals need more help."

I stick out a hand and say, "Thanks, I'm Daisy. I'm from Maine."

He covers my hand in his large, firm palm. "Jake from Alabama."

"And I'm Beastly from Senegal, but you knew that." She bats long eyelashes at Jake.

I crank an eyebrow at my roommate. "Aren't you, Lulu?"

That's the name of the person I signed a lease with for one year.

"Yes. Most of the time. But Beastly is my alternate persona. See how they go together?"

They're not even in the same universe, but I nod anyway.

Jake laughs. "Nice to meet you again, Lulu. And Daisy." He winks at me and turns to leave.

"We're having a party this weekend, Jake. Please come." Lulu bats her long, fluttery eyelashes again at him. It seems to be her signature move.

"We are?" I ask, staring at the door to the apartment I have yet to see.

"Of course. How will I welcome you and introduce you to my friends?"

"Thanks for the invite," Jake says.

"Please come," I find myself saying.

He turns his dimpled smile full force on me.

"Fine. It's a date."

Lulu—or Beastly—and I watch as handsome Jake trots down the stairs and enters his apartment.

"I can't believe I have a date," I say, dragging my suitcase to the door. "I haven't even been in Paris for a day."

"You sure work fast," Lulu says. "Stole that hot man right out from under my glittering eyelashes."

"I'm so sorry. I can't believe I begged a man I don't know to come hang out with me this weekend. It must be the jet lag. I'll tell him it was a mistake," I say hurriedly.

"Phooey. He's not my type. I invited him because he's here alone in Paris and doesn't know anyone."

"How do you know that?"

"Honey, I know everything."

"I bet."

"The thing I know the most is not to get in the way of love." She raises her eyebrows at me. Also glittery.

I give my bag one final tug and fall through the door. "I don't love Jake. I don't even know his last name."

Lulu picks my bag up easily with one hand and carries it the rest of the way in. Impressive muscles bulge in thick forearms.

"Details are not important," she says, swinging my giant bag like it's a picnic basket. "If we ignore the details, we'd all be much happier."

"But the details are what make us unique." I object, looking around the spacious apartment with the bird's eye view out the porthole windows at the Paris rooftops.

I get an urge to sing and dance like a Disney character.

"Not the *unimportant* details that people get hung up on. You know, like age, gender, ethnicity, those things."

"Right," I agree. "Irrelevant."

"Good. Glad we agree."

I eye Beastly/Lulu fully, taking in all of the glitter. "Um . . . do you mind me asking . . . what do you prefer I call you? Lulu or Beastly? And what are your preferred pronouns?"

The last thing I want to do is offend my roommate.

With hands on hips, my roomie smirks. "We just agreed it was irrelevant. Call me whatever you prefer."

"Okay, Lulu," I smile. "I like that name. What about your pronouns?"

My roomie blinks. "You Americans are so blunt. Where's the magic?"

"I'm sorry."

"I'm a work in progress. A magical work in progress!" Glitter goes flying as Lulu does a little twirl.

"Okay," I whisper. "I love magical anything."

Lulu sweeps her arm outward. "Good. If it makes it easier for you, I prefer she/hers. But let's move on to the grand tour."

My whole body feels aflame with embarrassment. Was I rude, demanding to know Lulu's personal information right off the bat?

Are Americans known as rude for this very reason?

Lulu grabs my arm. "Come on, my little Disney Princess, let me show you the view."

Lulu pushes on one of the windows. The entire thing swings open like a small *Alice in Wonderland* door.

"A secret portal," I exclaim.

"You can go out there. We have our own sky space."

"You mean a rooftop balcony?"

"Yes, rooftop. Skytop."

I stick my head through the doorway.

A loud noise buzzes next to my ears.

"What's out there?" I ask.

"Go look." Lulu's voice sparkles with mischief. "It's a surprise."

I hop carefully through the window/door, feeling like Alice on my way to the Mad Tea Party.

Chapter Six

DAISY

"I can see the Eiffel Tower," I squeal.

My jet lag disappears as I spin around the rooftop space, which is exclusively part of Lulu's and my apartment.

It's larger than the apartment itself. It feels like a secret garden nestled above the bustling heart of Paris.

Wrought-iron railings, delicate and ornate, edge the large space. The stone floor is weathered and chipped in some places. Vibrant green plants give off lavender and mint fragrances. A small, round bistro table and two wrought-iron chairs sit by the railing. I imagine this is where Lulu and I will sit with our coffees in the morning or wine in the evenings.

It has a perfect line of sight with the Eiffel Tower.

The wall of greenery is the showpiece, though, with its flowers hanging next to the balcony looking more like a floating garden from up here.

All around are sloping slate roofs and chimneys that seem close enough to touch. If we had to run through the city by rooftop we could start here.

No wonder Lulu wants to throw a party. With this space, it'll be fantastic.

The buzzing is the weed wacker of the gardener tending the vertical garden. He's perched on a gigantic crane/ladder with a harness around his waist.

He ignores me as I snap photos to send to my sisters.

A sky gardener. In Paris!

They won't believe how lucky I was to choose this place over the many others we'd researched online.

We'd looked at photos Lulu posted about the apartment, but she didn't post anything from up here.

"You left out the best part," I tell her when she comes out to join me. She had to fold herself in half to get through the small door.

She smiles. "There are hardly any surprises left in the world. You can see everything online. The way a person reacts to my surprise tells me a lot."

I scoop up my dress and spin around like Belle in *Beauty & the Beast*.

"And? How did I do?"

Lulu laughs. "We will get along just fine."

"*Magnifique*," I smile.

Lulu points out famous landmarks as I dance around humming, "*A Tale as Old as Time.*"

"You're really going to turn us into *Beauty & the Beast*."

"You started it," I tease.

"I can't believe you said you were shy and quiet in your emails."

"I usually am. But I don't know . . . I feel different here already."

"It's Paris," Lulu sighs. "I remember when I first arrived."

"From Senegal?" I ask, slowing down my twirling.

"From a small rural village in Senegal. I came here to attend school and be a teacher. But then . . . I became Paris. Or Paris became me."

"What does that mean?" I ask, longing to know.

Lulu puts a glittery fingernail to her chin. "It means you discover who you're meant to be in Paris. If you allow yourself. I found out I'm a doll dresser."

"A what?"

"A doll dresser. It's what I do. I create outfits for dolls. Someone has to do it."

"That's a job?"

Gosh, I sound rude as hell. But I can't stop my questions.

"It pays the rent. Well, mostly."

I twirl around the balcony. "That's the best thing I've ever heard."

Lulu smiles broadly. "Thanks. I've won awards for the best-dressed dolls. I'm waiting to hear back from a major company I applied to."

"Yes? What kind of position?"

"High fashion dolls. Expensive ones. It's a big thing."

"Oh, I hope you get it, Lulu."

I can't believe I'm so lucky to be rooming with a doll dresser. What a cool job.

"I hope I find my calling in Paris, too."

"You will. As long as you're true to what you love doing."

"I love love."

Lulu laughs. "Join the club, sweetheart."

"And writing about love," I add.

"You've come to the right place."

I walk around the rooftop slowly, sniffing the pine-scented aroma of the trees growing in the vertical garden.

"Do you have a boyfriend back home? Or a girlfriend? Someone special?" Lulu asks, curling up on her side on one of the chaise lounge chairs I hadn't noticed.

"No. I've never had a boyfriend."

Lulu's head shakes from side to side. "I don't believe that."

"It's true."

"What's wrong with the American boys in your state?"

"They liked my sister instead."

Lulu waves away my words. "Maybe you didn't want a boyfriend. Maybe you didn't think you were ready. Maybe you didn't like yourself enough."

"Huh?" I mumble, amazed at her directness.

"All reasons we don't have a special someone."

"I do like someone I met last year. But we're only friends. Or at least I thought we were friends." I can hear the sadness in my tone. "He was pretty special."

Lulu sits up and stretches her arms wide. "That's a start. What happened to him?"

I shrug. "He's traveling. But his family has an apartment in Paris. Maybe he'll come back."

Lulu stares hard at me. "We are not *waiting* for him, right? Because this weekend, you have a date with a hunky, American cowboy."

I didn't want to burst Lulu's bubble by telling her Alabama isn't cowboy territory.

"I'm not waiting," I say. "I'm living."

Lulu smiles widely. "I like you, Daisy Walker."

"Thanks, Lulu. I like you too."

"Okay, now let's figure out what we're having for dinner. Gorgeous doesn't just happen. We must eat right. And drink well."

Chapter Seven

DAISY

I yawn. "I don't know if I can stand up for much longer."

Lulu ignores my protests and tells me to go splash cold water on my face. "It's the remedy for everything."

When I reemerge on the balcony, washed and dressed in another floral dress, Lulu laughs. "I see I have my work cut out for me."

"What?" I spin around. "This is a vintage Laura Ashley."

She wrinkles up her nose. "Vintage fuddy-duddy, you mean."

I laugh happily. "You know our American slang."

She shrugs. "I've watched Queer Eye once or twice. We'll go shopping before the party. Paris vintage is like no other."

"I'm not wearing black," I say, crossing my arms.

"Of course not. You couldn't pull it off if you tried. We will find you a lovely minty green velvet mini dress with a curved neckline. Or maybe a crimson tulle that flares out when you dance. Trust me."

"Those sound weirdly specific. But beautiful."

"I'm conjuring them up in my mind right now! It's my job."

"My father gave me a credit card to buy new clothes. He said my mother would have insisted."

"Where's your mother?"

Lulu and I are climbing back through our portal. I have one foot on the rooftop and one inside the apartment.

It feels right that I'm caught between two places because that's how I feel whenever I think about Mom.

I am caught between being the brave little girl everyone said I should be.

"*Be strong for Emerald. She's your baby sister. She needs you to show her the way.*"

And the young woman who's afraid she'll fall apart, so she doesn't put herself out there.

"I was seven years old when she died."

What I don't say is that I think about Mom every day. I've never gotten over missing her, hearing her voice, seeing her smile. Can you ever get over something like that, though?

I look at my new friend, surprised to see tears forming in her eyes.

"Mine, too," she says softly. "When I was ten."

My giant of a friend suddenly looks like a broken doll.

We don't say anything as we walk down the four flights of stairs to the front door and into the still-warm evening air of my first night in Paris.

I've heard people say that the light in Paris is different somehow.

And stepping out into the street, I have to agree.

The sky is glowy, soft, and fragrant with the perfumes of all the Parisians walking home with their baguettes and pastries from the boulangeries.

I take my new roommate's arm.

"My mom would have been glad I met you," I say. "That I'm in Paris with you."

Lulu pulls off her colorful silk scarf and slips it around my neck.

She ties the flimsy material into the perfect French accessory with two quick turns of her large wrists.

It flutters in the breeze as we walk past the cafes, which are filling up. Their braided red and cream chairs with circular backs and tiny tables look like photographs of Paris come to life.

"I can't believe I'm here," I say, a smile bursting across my face. My heart has gone from sad to joyous in a split second.

"It's Paris. *C'est la vie*!"

"*Oui! C'est la vie,*" I say to no one and everyone.

Speaking a few French words makes me feel like I'm fitting in a tiny bit. Even if all I'm saying is, "Yes, this is life."

"*Merci*," I tell a passerby who says something in French after bumping into me.

Lulu hoots. "You just told that man 'thank you' for hitting you.

A familiar flush courses through my body.

We're walking the famous Rue Montorgueil. It's a pedestrian-only zone, with shops and restaurants lined up on either side of the road. Vintage signs adorn some buildings, like a baker over a boulangerie and grapes over a wine shop.

"Maybe that's what I meant," I say boldly, catching the eye of a man walking straight toward me.

He smiles. I smile back. It's like I'm this girl . . . no, woman, I don't recognize. Someone bolder, braver, and even a bit flirtatious.

Lulu shakes her head. Her long, flowing hair, which I suspect is a very expensive wig, ripples behind her.

"You're going to have a lot of people hurting once I unleash those sexy curves of yours to the world."

My mouth drops open in surprise.

I try to eyeball my roomie, but she's too tall for me to do anything but poke her arm.

"What sexy curves? Are you saying I'm fat?" I grab my stomach, which has never revealed one single ab in its entire life. "I mean, I'm chubby . . . I'm not like my sisters who are all . . . ."

Lulu grabs my arm before I can finish.

"Shush, my glorious swan who thinks she's an ugly duckling. Have you *seen* your dimples and slanted brown eyes? Or that bosom that would make Marilyn Monroe envious?"

"But my sisters . . . they're so beautiful," I stutter.

"But are they in Paris?" Lulu twirls me around in the middle of the street.

No one bats an eyelash as if it's normal for a glittery giant and a chubby American dressed like a *Little House on the Prairie* character to dance in front of century-old buildings where the French have been buying their beef, wine, and bread for centuries.

"*Merci*," I shout to Lulu, who towers above my head.

"*De rien*," she says, spinning me one more time.

I hope Lulu can feel all the weight of my gratitude in my smile.

Chapter Eight

LEO

"You live in an actual castle?" James asks as the large black limousine stops in front of the arched entranceway. "With actual turrets?!"

I grin, taking in the familiar sight. "Welcome to Arandel."

Thank goodness I changed my clothes before arriving. Our Chief Butler had sent a complete royal ensemble with tails and everything on the jet.

I swapped my jeans and sweatshirt for the formalwear in the back of the plane as James rolled his eyes.

After I was dressed, he sighed and pulled out a gorgeous leopard cape from the bottom of one of his bags. Like it was no big deal.

It was made for him. The leopard had died of natural causes, he had informed me the first time I saw it and was horrified.

We were ten years old. I wore knee socks; his leopard cape hung to his ankles. Guess who was cooler?

In the jet, James swung the cape across his broad shoulders.

Now, it hangs to his waist. Then he tied a rolled-up leopard headband around the crown of his head.

It's been the traditional wear of his Zulu Nation royals for a long time.

He wears it only on special state occasions.

"You're missing the spear," I say seriously because it *is* part of his royal clothing.

"It's in my other bag in the cargo hold. I won't forget it."

James and I met in boarding school when we were ten years old. I've been around him when he was in full Zulu royal wear, elaborate feathers and all, and it made me look like his servant.

"Way to outshine me on my home turf, dude," I said admiringly after our plane landed, and our chauffeur was more impressed with James than with seeing me again.

"We are the People of the Heavens," he reminded me. The cape rose and fell with his movements. It was stunning, even matched with his black and white Vans.

"Right. Maybe leave the spear in your bag," I suggested.

"You think?" he raised a wicked eyebrow. He put a hand to his chin. "It might impress the girls, though."

"There are no girls," I said. "Don't speak to Olivia."

He raised both hands. "I promise."

Kingdom of Arandel

The grand iron gates creak open, revealing the sweeping driveway with lush, manicured gardens.

I glance over at James and catch the moment his eyes widen, taking in the sprawling estate.

The castle looms in the distance, its three majestic turrets piercing the sky like crowns atop the ancient stone structure.

"What do you think?" I ask, nudging him as the car comes to a slow halt at the foot of the stone staircase.

He lets out a low whistle. "I think you should've warned me, Leo. This is more of a kingdom than a home."

I step out of the car. "Well, technically, it is."

We walk side by side toward the towering entrance, where two royal guards in crisp uniforms swing open the massive double doors leading into the main hall.

I sneak a glance at James, waiting for his reaction.

As a Zulu prince, he's no stranger to opulence, but I know our Arandel Castle will still impress.

His eyes scan the high, vaulted ceilings adorned with intricate carvings, the light streaming through the stained-glass windows casting soft shades of blue and gold on the stone floors.

"Not bad, huh?" I say, my tone playful, though I can't help feeling a hint of pride.

"Not bad?" James gives a little laugh.

I'm about to respond when soft footsteps echo through the hall. We both turn as my mother, Queen Isabelle of Arandel, appears at the top of the grand staircase.

She descends with her usual grace, revealing a lifetime in the public eye in every step. Her silver hair is pinned back and decorated with a jeweled tiara. Her emerald-green gown sweeps the floor as she moves.

"Mother." I want to run to her and ask if Father is okay. But I know she expects me to act like the trained royal I am.

I smile and step forward. "There's someone I'd like you to meet."

Her face is free from lines of worry. But I know it's part of the facade—the careful hiding of one's emotions.

She bows her head in deference to the Zulu prince.

"Welcome to Arandel, your Royal Highness." Her voice is smooth and welcoming, but I don't miss the heaviness beneath it.

James steps forward, inclining his head in a respectful bow. "Your Majesty, it's an honor to meet you finally. Leo has spoken very highly of you."

My mother's smile softens as she extends her hand, but I can see the distant worry in her eyes, even though she's trying to hide it.

"The pleasure is mine, Prince James. My son has told me many stories of your adventures together."

James takes her hand and says, smooth as butter, "I hope he's told you only the good parts."

My mother chuckles, but the sound doesn't quite reach her eyes. "I'm sure you two have caused more mischief than he lets on," she teases, her gaze flicking briefly to me. I catch the unspoken message, the familiar tension slipping back in between us.

I clear my throat, the ease of the moment fading. "Shall we head to the garden?" I ask, trying to shake off the weight pressing down on me. "It's still early enough to enjoy the sunshine."

Chapter Nine

LEO

The Queen nods. As she turns to lead us down the corridor, her voice softens, almost inaudible. "Leo, after tea, we must talk."

My stomach clenches. I know what's coming, but I push the thought aside, forcing a smile for James's sake. "Wait until you see the gardens. You'll never want to leave."

From the look on James's face, I know he wants to laugh. We never speak to each other formally except . . . well, never. So, me saying he'll love the gardens is like a step into a Twilight Zone for us. But he's a professional royal and will go along. I don't have to worry.

As we make our way through the sunlit halls, the air between my mother and me grows heavier with every step. James pretends to be unaware of the tension as he marvels at the beauty of the castle.

I know better. He's been raised to deflect and misdirect better than most.

I do my own internal misdirecting by sending my thoughts toward Daisy.

How is she enjoying Paris. Where is she staying? It's been months since I last saw her in Porto, but the ache in my chest never seems to dull.

I'd do anything to escape my royal duties and catch the next flight to Paris.

But how could I? When my father is dying. And my mother looks overwhelmed with grief.

We enter the garden and head straight for the table set for tea.

The Queen gestures for James to sit. For a few minutes, we chat about nothing. Peacocks parade their feathers across the lawn. James whispers that he'd like to get one of their feathers as a souvenir. "If Olivia would allow it."

I normally would respond with a smart remark, but I bite my tongue. It's not the time or place to be joking with James.

"James, please enjoy yourself," Mother says softly, her voice polite. "I need a moment with Leo."

James nods and rises from his seat. "I'll take a stroll. This garden is incredible."

"Stay away from my peacocks," I say, a demand I never thought I'd ever hear myself say.

"I'll try," James says, patting my arm.

When he's out of earshot, I turn to my mother, "How is father? Can I see him?"

The Queen sighs, her gaze falling on the roses lining the garden. "His condition is worsening. The physicians don't believe he will see the next spring. You must start preparing—"

"No way," I cut in. "I want to see him."

I can't believe I'm going to lose my father. I also can't believe I'll have to be King so soon.

I stand abruptly, pacing to the edge of the garden, running a hand through my hair. "I'm not ready to be king, Mother. I thought I had more time. I thought—"

"None of us expected this," she interrupts. She rises and walks over to me, her hand resting lightly on my arm. "But time is not on our side. You are the Crown Prince. The kingdom will need you when your father . . . ."

I ask the question that's been swirling inside me like a storm. "What about Leif?"

She inhales sharply. "He's studying."

"I know. In Paris."

"Yes, where you were supposed to be."

I nod. I don't tell her that I'd have given up my gap year if I'd known Dad's cancer was going to return. I'd have stayed here and spent more time with him. Even though I wouldn't have met Daisy if I did.

"I mean . . . what about Leif for . . . ."

Mother shakes her head. "You are the firstborn."

"By fifteen minutes," I argue. "Leif has just as much right to be king as I do."

"Fate says no," she says, calling upon the one thing I could never argue with my parents about. They've always insisted that fate and destiny are like my godparents or something.

"It's your destiny to be king. Fate chose you."

I sigh heavily. "Leif wants it more than I do."

A frown creases her forehead. "I know."

"Is there something you're not telling me?"

"Have you spoken to Leif recently?"

I shake my head. "Not for lack of trying. He doesn't respond to my calls or texts."

She blinks. "What happened between you two?"

I look away. James is petting Bruce Banner, my English sheepdog, who's as large as the Incredible Hulk but ironically the sweetest, calmest dog.

"Fifteen minutes," I sigh. "Fifteen damn minutes is what happened between us."

Kingdom of Arandel

Chapter Ten

LEO

"Well, you need to fix whatever is wrong," Mother says fiercely. "Your father needs both of you by his side, and soon."

"Is it really going to be soon?" I swallow hard, the words catching in my throat. I sound like a little boy, not a man who's supposed to be king.

I can't bear the thought of my father dying. He's only in his mid-50s and, until recently, full of energy—chopping logs for the fireplace as if we don't have an official Groundskeeper or royal Woodcutter to do that for us.

"What if I'm not the right person for this?"

"You are," Mother whispers, her voice firm with the belief she's always had in me. "You must believe that."

I close my eyes for a moment, but when I open them, all I can think about is Daisy.

What would she think of me if I became king? Would I ever be free to see her again, or would duty keep us apart forever?

I long to be in Paris with her, walking along the Seine, holding her hand, losing myself in her world.

"There's someone I can't stop thinking about," I finally confess.

Mother glances over at James, who's still playing with Bruce Banner, giving us space.

"He seems like a nice young man."

I wave a hand in front of her eyes.

"No, Mother. James is my best friend. The person I'm talking about is Daisy Walker. She's an American girl, but she's in Paris for a few months. Maybe a year."

I hesitate to say more as I watch my mother's face fight a deepening frown.

"An American girl?"

"Yes."

I gather all my courage and say, "I want to see her again."

The moment the words are out of my mouth, I know they're the truest thing I've spoken in a long while.

All the years of saying the "right" thing, of being polite and understanding, of fitting into this image of the "future king"—fly out the window, or rather, out of the garden.

I reach for my mother's arm. "Let's walk so I can tell you about her."

"James," I call. "We're going to stroll the grounds. Care to join us?"

James and Bruce Banner come loping over as one. "I see you've found a new buddy," I say, stroking Bruce Banner's ears. He licks my hand.

"This is the best-behaved dog I've ever met," James exclaims.

Mother smiles tightly. "He's the royal pet, of course he's well-behaved."

James and I exchange glances.

"Of course, Your Highness."

He all but curtsies to my mother, and I smother a laugh.

This isn't the time for jokes. I have some serious convincing to do. It's like when I persuaded my parents to let me roam around the world with a surfboard for a year.

But now it's even more urgent than my freedom. It's my heart at stake.

"Daisy Walker is my soulmate. I knew it from the moment I met her in Porto."

Mother studies me for a long moment, her expression softens with understanding.

"Leo, love is a wonderful thing, but you cannot abandon your responsibilities. The kingdom needs you now more than ever."

I exhale, torn between my heart and my duty. I know what I must do, but that doesn't mean I'm ready to give up Daisy completely.

The scent of roses fills the air, but it does nothing to soothe the tension building in my chest.

Mother's voice rises. "It's not just your duty to be king. There's more."

"What more?" My eyes narrow.

"Leo, you must start thinking about a Queen."

"A Queen?" I almost choke on my words.

"You need to marry eventually. The sooner the better," she says softly but firmly, her gaze unwavering.

Bruce Banner breaks his royal behavior and barks loudly as if protesting for me.

I run my fingers through his thick fur. "It's okay, boy," I say. But it isn't.

"Excuse me," James says. "How soon is the Queen thinking?"

"It would be ideal if Leopold was at least engaged to be married by his coronation."

"That's less than one year away!" I feel my eyes opening wide as saucers.

"It's always been this way."

She turns to me. "We thought—your father and I—that you

would have more time, but with his condition . . . ." Her voice falters for a moment. "You no longer have the luxury of waiting to fall in love."

The words hit me like a blow. *Marry. Within a year?*

James let out a loud, unroyal whistle. "Is it required?"

Bruce Banner barks.

I grab the feet of the statue behind me waiting on her answer.

"No," Mother shakes her head. "It is not required. But why wait? Don't you want your father at your royal wedding?"

"I'm not made of stone, Mother. I can't marry just anyone."

Ironically, the cold stone statue I'm holding onto is of myself.

If I thought I wasn't ready to be king, I sure as hell am not prepared to be a husband to some stranger.

Chapter Eleven

DAISY

The morning sun lights up the narrow street as I step out of my apartment building, pulling my light sweater closer against the crisp Paris air.

After our dinner and glasses of wine last night, Lulu and I stayed up chatting about our lives until I could no longer keep my eyes open.

Now, the scent of fresh croissants and roasting coffee drifts from the nearby cafés, waking me up fully.

It reminds me of the café where Leo worked in Porto. On my first day there, Leo assembled a selection of delicious pastries for me since I couldn't decide for myself.

Pushing thoughts of Leo aside, I squeeze into one of the tiny tables on the sidewalk and order in French.

"Un café et deux croissants, s'il vous plaît."

The server looks as if he's wincing.

"Je suis désolée," I say, hoping that saying "I'm sorry" makes up for my terrible accent.

I'm rewarded with a big smile.

The server brings my coffee and two croissants quickly. I sit back, people-watching and enjoying my first morning in the City of Lights.

The street soon grows crowded with people—tourists with cameras, students riding bicycles, business people in suits and briefcases hurrying just like in New York, but better dressed.

I text Bridget in Greece and Corrine in Portugal since we are in, or close to, the same time zone now. Both sisters bomb my phone with heart and kiss emojis, and I laugh out loud.

It feels weird to sit here doing nothing but watching my surroundings, but it's what they do here, according to Lulu. It's the French way.

"I love being French." I type out to Bridget and Corrine.

"Oh la la!" Bridget texts back.

"Yummy French kissing," Corrine texts with a winky face.

I groan. My sisters are so corny.

I slide my phone away so I can focus on the view. Nobody is trying to hurry me after I finish eating.

I could probably drink wine right now, and nobody would care.

The empty seat next to my tiny table mocks me, though. I imagine Leo sitting in it and us talking about this and that: like what I'm writing or what he's doing in South Africa besides surfing.

I would talk about my sisters, as usual. He could tell me about his family.

Hmmmm . . . I don't know anything about his family. He mainly shared his day-to-day life with me. We texted daily for months, and I'm clueless about where he lives.

There was so much else to discuss. I thought we had a lot of time.

When I told Lulu I was not waiting on him but living my life, I meant it. But I can't help when thoughts of him creep into my mind.

It's been months since he disappeared from my life, as quickly as he had come into it.

The laughter we shared, the late-night phone calls, the way he'd tilt his head just slightly when he was really listening. And yet, it's like he never existed at all. No texts. No calls. Just . . . gone.

I shake off the horrible feeling of rejection and pay the bill. I have so much to see before my first class.

I focus on the path ahead. I won't let thoughts about a guy who ghosted me ruin the beauty of this morning.

My notebook is tucked under my arm, and I plan to spend the morning walking through the city, capturing the city's highlights in my own words.

Maybe if I immerse myself in the art and energy of Paris, I can finally shake the hollow ache in my chest.

My feet carry me through the winding streets of Paris, past centuries-old bookstores and cafés.

I cross the bustling Boulevards and wind my way down to the river, where the shimmering waters of the Seine glitter in the sunlight.

The Pont des Arts bridge appears before me, its iron railings adorned with thousands of locks—symbols of love left behind by couples from all over the world.

I pause at the entrance to the bridge, my heart tugging with a bittersweet pang. I've never had a special someone to lock my heart to. I mean, I would have with Leo, but look how that turned out.

I smack the railing hard and hurt my hand. Serves me right.

I watch as the grey-green Seine water swirls past under the bridge. I trace my fingers over the cool metal of the locks, reading the initials carved into them and imagining the stories behind each one.

Couples who stood where I stand now, full of hope and joy, believing that their love would last forever.

I smile despite myself, feeling real happiness for them.

I stop in the middle of the bridge, my gaze drifting again to the water below.

What would it be like to stand here with Leo and lock a symbol of our love on this very bridge?

Would we laugh and say it's so corny? Or would we be serious and carve our initials into the metal so it's clear whose hearts we were joining together as one?

I shake my head. "Don't be ridiculous, Daisy; Leo is far, far away from here. You promised you were no longer going to live in a dream world. You are going to live in the moment!"

"Excuse me, mademoiselle, are you okay?" A deep guttural voice asks. "You're not thinking of jumping, are you?"

"What?" I gasp. "*Non*," I say firmly in French. I step back from the edge of the bridge where the locks are clamped. It's funny how the tokens of love are in the most dangerous spots.

I turn to see a young man, probably in his mid-twenties, wearing a bright orange city worker's vest and carrying a clipboard.

He's studying the locks closely, making notes, occasionally shaking his head.

Curiosity gets the better of me, and I step closer. "*Bonjour*," I greet him with a small smile, my French hesitant.

He looks up, offering a polite smile in return. "Bonjour, mademoiselle."

"What are you doing?" I ask, nodding toward the locks.

"Ah," he says, glancing back at the railing. "I'm assessing the locks. The city is concerned that they're getting too heavy for the bridge. They may have to be removed soon."

I brush away the long hair that's flying in my eyes. "Removed? But . . . they're symbols of love."

He nods. "I know. Many people feel the same way. But the weight is starting to affect the structure. The bridge wasn't designed to hold so many locks. There are thousands here, and more are added every day."

I look at the sea of locks, my heart sinking a little. It's hard to imagine this iconic part of Paris being stripped away.

"That's . . . sad," I murmur. "All these stories, all these couples who believed their love would last forever."

The worker glances at me. "Love isn't about a lock on a bridge, mademoiselle. It's about what happens after you walk away from it. If it's true, it doesn't need a lock to keep it alive."

I blink, caught off guard by his words.

For a moment, I stand in silence, absorbing what he's said. It's not about the lock. It's about the love itself, the kind that transcends tokens and symbols.

But what about when the person you love vanishes? When they leave you alone on a bridge.

"Maybe you're right," I say softly.

The young man gives me a kind nod before turning back to his clipboard. "I'm sorry, but the decision may be made soon. The locks might have to go. If you know some couples who put them here, you can let them know. Or if you have someone special, there are other ways to remember them."

I thank him and continue my walk across the bridge, my fingers brushing the locks one last time.

As I reach the other side, I pause and look back, the weight of the locks reflecting the weight in my heart.

Leo walked away from me before we even had a chance to see if there was something between us.

There must be something I can do to save other people's true love, even if I could not save my own.

Chapter Twelve

DAISY

I slide into the wooden seat smack dab in the middle of the lecture hall like I'm at the movie theater and want the best view.

My first day at the Sorbonne. Just the thought of it is enough to make my heart race.

I look around at the other students—some chatting excitedly, others scrolling on their phones or flipping through textbooks.

The room is large, old, and full of history. I feel like I've already been here, maybe in another life.

Everything looks and feels familiar. I should be in a bright blue dress with a corset and my curls twisted and pinned in a Marie Antoinette hairstyle.

Instead of a floral dress and a tangle of curls trailing down my back, with a brightly flushed face from running here after my love lock detour on the bridge.

Students open their laptops and talk amongst themselves.

I set my notebook down and pull out my pen with a flourish. I can't believe I get to take European Art History in a city where so much great art was created.

"Did you forget your laptop?" A girl two seats away asks kindly.

"No, I love writing." I tap my pen on the table for emphasis.

She gasps. The look of horror on her face makes me giggle.

"A modern laptop seems out of place here. Or maybe it's me who is out of place," I say.

She shrugs her slim shoulders. Dressed in a black jacket over a creamy shirt, she has a classic French simplicity. Another "look" I couldn't pull off, as Lulu would say.

I gaze around to see if anyone else is writing with an old-fashioned pen.

That's when my eyes catch on someone a few rows ahead and to the left of me. A young man, handsome in a quiet, almost brooding way, is slumped in his chair.

His dark hair is slightly tousled, and from where I'm sitting, I see his sharp jawline. It's blocked whenever a lock of hair falls across his face. He sweeps it back impatiently like he wants to take scissors to it but keeps forgetting.

"Whoa," I mutter under my breath.

Except I'm not as quiet as I thought.

The girl near me chuckles. "Étienne De la Bastide. Welcome to his fan club."

I feel the telltale redness creeping up my skin. Thank goodness my brown skin covers it a little.

"Who is Étienne De la Bastide?" I ask.

She flicks her fingers in the young man's direction. "Only one of France's most up-and-coming artists. He's already had his own solo show. He must be taking this class as a requirement."

She stops talking when the professor enters and drops a stack of books on the desk in front of the classroom.

"I'm Maxine," the girl side-whispers.

"Daisy Walker," I say.

"Like the flower?" Maxine asks, one eyebrow cocked.

"Exactly like the flower," I smile. "And he's beautiful."

"So are you," Maxine says in a matter-of-fact way, which almost makes me believe her.

The professor clears his throat loudly.

He speaks in French. I stop fangirling and pay attention.

My French is good enough to order food and get me around, but not good enough to grasp the nuances of art history.

Thank God for the English subtitles appearing on a screen behind the professor's head.

That is where my eyes are glued for the rest of the class except whenever Étienne moves a muscle.

I WATCH, FASCINATED WHENEVER HIS LONG FINGERS move across the page of his sketchbook. While everyone else seems focused on the professor, Étienne is drawing, completely absorbed in his world.

There's something magnetic about him—the way his brow furrows in concentration and the way his hand glides across the page. He isn't paying the slightest bit of attention to the lecture that's just begun, and it makes me smile to myself.

When the professor begins explaining how the Impressionist artists launched a revolutionary new art movement in Paris in the late 1800s, I try to focus. I really do.

But every few minutes, my eyes drift back to the young man. His sketching never stops, and I wonder what he's drawing.

What thoughts are running through *his* mind? He seems so serious, so unreachable.

A loud screeching noise goes off in my head.

He's unreachable, Daisy. You already have one of these unavailable men in your life—no need to reach for another.

"Oh, hush," I say in my head.

I struggle to focus on the professor who's discussing the difference between the Romantics and the Impressionists.

The class moves on, and the professor's voice becomes background noise to my wandering thoughts.

I came to Paris determined to live my dream, to immerse myself in a world of art, writing, food, and culture.

And—maybe most importantly—to finally fall in love. This is Paris, the city of romance. If there's ever a place to experience first love, it's here. And with Leo gone, it's time to meet someone new.

"That's what you keep saying like a broken record," my inner voice shouts. *"I bet you don't have the nerve to talk to Étienne."*

I sink deeper into my seat as the screen darkens then fills with images of gorgeous, colorful paintings. Famous paintings by famous painters from when they lived in Paris.

There's Vincent Van Gogh. Matisse. Gauguin and Monet.

I watch Étienne's shoulders pull back as he lifts his head. For the first time since class started, he's paying attention.

I soon forget about Étienne, about writing notes, about everything, as I fall under the spell of the heart-stopping, beautiful images cascading around me.

The images fill the entire room, the ceiling, and the walls. We are inside the paintings, and it is magnificent.

My breath catches, and tears form in my eyes at the flowers dancing in a magical light around me.

"La lumière est tout." The professor clicks back on the overhead light.

"Light is everything," I translate.

I thought I had whispered it, but apparently, I said it aloud. People turn toward me. Even Étienne looks in my direction.

I feel my skin flaming like someone has lit *me* up from inside.

That's when I see the tiny smile forming at the corners of his perfect lips.

He raises a hand, and the professor calls his name. Now, everyone turns their attention to him.

Thank goodness.

Étienne says in flawless English, "It is the fleeting quality of light, just like the fleeting nature of love, that makes all the difference."

He snaps his long fingers. "Even the light in a person's skin tone must be captured just right."

"Exactement," the professor says proudly.

Étienne nods in my direction.

"Is he talking about me?"

As if he's heard my silent question, he nods yes.

"Oh my goodness, he's into you," Maxine squeals.

I blush harder. Maxine may look classy and cool, but she sounds like one of my sisters. Embarrassing!

"Hush, he'll hear you. And no way."

She reaches over and squeezes my hand. "Let me touch the arm of the woman who captured Étienne de la Bastide's eye."

"Okay, don't go crazy," I whisper. "He barely looked over here."

But that isn't true. My skin is still feeling the effects of his eyes on me. And it feels like I'm on a roller coaster ride going all the way up, cresting at the top and ready to fall.

Chapter Thirteen

DAISY

As the lecture changes direction and the professor discusses what's expected of us this year, I glance at my notebook and realize I haven't written much of anything.

I frantically scribble down notes about what is upcoming. I try to keep my eyes from straying over in Étienne's direction.

When the final bell rings and the students begin to gather their things, I can't help it. My eyes dart to the young artist again.

He's closing his sketchbook, his expression unreadable, his movements slow and deliberate.

Without thinking, I stand up quickly and tell Maxine I will see her in our next session.

Then, gathering my books, I step down a few rows toward him.

My heart thuds nervously in my chest, but I push it aside. This is Paris, and I'm not going to let this opportunity slip by.

"Hi," I say softly, offering Étienne a tentative smile as I approach.

The young man looks up, surprised for a moment, his dark eyes meeting mine. Up close, he's even more striking, his features sharp but softened by the slight stubble on his chin. He doesn't say anything at first, but he gives me a small nod of acknowledgment.

I bite my lip and hold up my notebook. "I noticed you were sketching during the lecture. If you need the notes, I'd be happy to share them with you."

For a moment, he looks at me as if he's studying me the same way he'd been studying his sketchbook.

Then, a small smile like the one he gave me before tugs at the corner of his lips. It's not much, but it's enough to make my stomach do a tiny flip.

"Thanks," he says, his voice low, with his French accent. "That's nice of you."

My heart skips a beat. I hadn't expected him to speak so softly, as though he's carefully choosing his words.

I glance at the sketchbook under his arm. "You're an artist?"

Gosh, Daisy, how lame? I can hear Emerald's criticism in my head.

He hesitates for a second, then gives a slight nod. "Something like that."

"I'd love to see what you're working on," I offer, my nerves buzzing but my determination stronger.

"I'm Daisy, by the way. The girl with the 'light.'" In my nervousness, I do silly air quotes.

He looks at me for a long moment as if deciding whether or not to share more, and then finally replies, "I'm Étienne."

"Nice to meet you, Étienne." I can't stop myself from smiling now. He's quiet, almost mysterious, but there's something about his reserved nature that intrigues me. "I guess you're not really interested in art history, huh?"

Étienne's small smile returns. "It's not that. I just . . . prefer to learn by creating."

My smile widens. "That's a good way to learn." I hesitate for a second, then add, "Well, if you ever want to compare notes—or sketches—let me know."

Étienne gives a slight nod, his expression still thoughtful, but the way his eyes linger on me tells me that maybe—just maybe—there's a connection here.

As I turn to leave, I can't help but feel a rush of excitement. Paris is already starting to work its magic.

"Hey, do you want to come to a party? My roommate and I are hosting one this Friday on our amazing wraparound balcony."

This mad deluge of words tumble out of my mouth.

"I mean, if you would like to. It's not a date. Just an invite. And the light there is fantastic. You could even draw."

"Shut up, Daisy," I shout at myself.

The beautiful young man with the sharp features and long, slim drawing fingers breaks into a real smile, then a grin. Dimples flash and I am smitten.

"*Oui.*"

"*Oui?*" I ask. He said *yes?!*

"I would love to come—me and my sketchpad." He raises the pad in the air above his chest.

I screw up my eyes. "Awkward?"

"A bit. But it's because you think I can draw . . . I'm horrible."

"No. Not true."

"We'll see," he says quietly. He scribbles his number on the edge of my notebook page. "Text me the address."

My heart is tripping big time. I asked a guy out on a date. I mean, not a date. I asked him to a party.

A handsome, talented artist guy.

A memory of Leo's face flits through my consciousness, threatening to rip my heart out again.

I shut it down fast.

Nope. I am moving on.

And with Étienne's quiet smile still in my mind, I feel like I might just be on my way.

Chapter Fourteen

LEO

I've never defied my parents. I've always understood my role here. But I never thought I'd have to marry someone I didn't love and . . . didn't even know.

In the distance, I can see the river that flows through our land. It reminds me of the Douro River in Porto, where Daisy and I walked along the banks marveling at the boats that carried kegs of wine from up the valley.

I can still hear her laughter and the way she spoke of her dreams to be a writer.

I told her I was traveling to see the world and surf the seven seas.

She didn't think it was pretentious or a waste of time, which are both things that Leif called my gap year.

My heart aches for her. When her sister Corrine had relationship troubles with Salvador Torres, Portugal's premier footballer, I was right there by Daisy's side, helping her to help her sister and Salvador save their love.

Now it feels like my turn. I need to save my relationship with Daisy.

Although I'm the one who turned my back on it. How wrong I was. The worst mistake I ever made.

Back in the castle, everything feels gloomy and sad. The palace walls, the lingering scent of polished wood and lavender in the halls, and most of all, the silent weight of my father's illness.

It's a constant undercurrent here, running beneath every conversation, every glance exchanged with my mother, every hushed whisper from the palace staff.

I thank James for hanging around with me. He promises he'll stay as long as I need him.

I sit beside my father's bed, the mornings still dark as the days grow shorter.

His face is pale, his eyes duller than I remember, but they light up with that familiar glint whenever I enter the room. It makes everything inside me knot up.

"Are you comfortable, Father?" I ask, pouring him a cup of tea. I know he can't drink much of it, but the habit grounds me.

"Perfectly, my son," he answers, his voice thinner than before. "Come, tell me what you've been reading lately."

We settle into the familiar rhythm. I read to him from one of his favorite history books, though the words blur as I go along.

I'm doing my best to keep my voice steady, to ignore the rasp in his breathing, and to hold back every bitter word I'd like to spit at fate.

But he listens, watching me with a small, approving smile. For those brief moments, it's almost as if nothing has changed.

Later, I meet with some of our ministers, discussing trade negotiations and preparations for the upcoming winter.

Their eyes on me are sharp as if checking for cracks in my abilities, which, trust me, they won't find.

They may think of me as the rebellious surfer, but swimming in cold waters with sharks and riding waves takes cool, calm, discipline and tenacity, traits that will help me as King.

James and I both agreed on that when we chose to be surfers.

I am Crown Prince, and with Father's condition, I hope they all begin to see me as the man who will soon be their capable king. I know they want me to prove I can carry the weight.

By evening, I find myself seated across from my mother with James at my right at dinner. She's always dressed elegantly, her posture impeccable as she lifts her gaze and studies me with that sharp, discerning look she's perfected over the years.

James talks about his visits to the surrounding villages and his tours of our factories.

Mother never fails to bring up my future wife. This evening, she takes it a step further by bringing up a royal ball.

"Leo," she begins, and I can feel a shift in the air. "You know the importance of stability for our kingdom. We need to ensure you are settled, that you have a partner who can stand beside you when your time comes to rule."

I lean back, trying to keep my expression neutral. "Mother, I'm here to help Father recover, not to plan parties."

Her lips tighten, but she pushes forward. "Your father is ill, yes, but this was his idea. He wishes to see you secure before . . . ." She trails off, leaving the implication hanging heavily between us.

"A ball would be the perfect opportunity for you to meet some of the noblewomen and perhaps . . . consider their potential as a partner."

"You want me to host a ball *now*?" I ask, unable to hide the bite in my tone. "With Father so ill?"

She pulls in her lips and drops her gaze. I catch a rare glimpse of her pain in her slumped shoulders. Mother's posture is always perfect.

"I apologize," I tell her.

"This is what he wants. We both want to see you settled, Leo. You have a duty to this family, to this kingdom."

She starts listing possible candidates—noblewomen, daughters of ministers, and even a foreign princess. I try to listen, I really do, but every name she mentions blurs together in my mind. I feel a pressure building in my chest, squeezing until it's almost unbearable.

I'm here, in Arandel, fulfilling my duties as son and prince. Yet it feels wrong. Empty. Like I'm slipping into a life that belongs to someone else.

But I owe them this. I owe my father his peace, and my mother her hopes for a stable throne. So I nod, swallowing the urge to protest. "If this is what he wants . . . we'll plan a ball."

Her face relaxes, a brief smile touching her lips. "Good. You'll see, Leo. A proper partner will make all the difference. Soon, you'll wonder how you ever doubted this path."

I force a small smile, but inside, all I can think of is Daisy—her laughter echoing in my memory, her fierce independence, the way she felt that love was our superpower.

And now, here I am about to give my superpower away as a party favor.

Kingdom of Arandel

Chapter Fifteen

LEO

The ball is set for mid-December, a Christmas Ball, three months away. There is plenty of time to organize the event, but Mother says that invitations must be sent out at least two months before such a major event.

The palace is alive with preparations. As if everyone is excited to be doing something celebratory after so much pain and worry.

It's the kind of energy I haven't felt at home in years. Tailors bustle in and out, arms loaded with fabrics in deep emeralds and royal blues. They measure and poke me and James, making us feel like living mannequins.

Gamekeepers from the estate are busy securing wild boar, venison, and pheasant to put in the freezer.

Plants and flowers are brought in and placed in the greenhouses. They arrive from every corner of Arandel, along with the most delicate crystal candelabras, lace table linens, and dozens of arrangements to decorate the ballroom.

Father and I share an afternoon tea several times a week on the days he feels better and his spirits are lighter. He jokes about how all this fuss reminds him of his own youth and of the splendor of royal gatherings when he was a boy.

"It's been too long since we've held a celebration here, Leo. And to celebrate you . . . ." He grips my hand, his voice filled with pride.

I feel like an ungrateful dog for doubting he has my best interests at heart. He and Mother both do. I know that.

"Father," I say, not wanting to linger on sentiment. "You're the only one who could convince me to do this."

He chuckles, a sound that fades into a light cough. "You're my son, Leo. You're ready for this."

I manage a small smile, relieved to see him at peace. Even my mother, who is more animated than ever, watches me with something that almost feels like pride.

Every evening, when James and I are watching Netflix or playing chess, I find myself scrolling through photos of me and Daisy in Porto.

Daisy's face and the memories pull me in, like a current I can't fight. Sometimes I think about the lives we could have had if we'd —if *I'd* had the courage to stay in touch with her. Instead of tearing us in two.

The crisp air settles like a mantle on my shoulders as I pace through the castle's south gardens. James has gone into town with our driver to check out Arandel's nightlife. We've been here for two weeks and he says he needs to meet more of Arandel's citizens.

I know he means female citizens.

Rows of tall, regal oaks stand like silent guardians around me, casting long shadows in the fading light.

The scent of freshly turned earth lingers as I walk, restless, tugging at my collar. Just ahead, I catch a glimpse of Father seated on the bench overlooking the rose garden. He's wrapped in his favorite wool coat, a scarf bundled around his neck, leaning slightly forward as if he's lost in thought. I hesitate, then take a breath, walking toward him.

"Leo," he says, a soft smile lifting the lines around his eyes when he notices me. "Are you just escaping your mother's ball preparations, or is something truly weighing on your mind?"

I smile briefly but can't quite hold it. "Maybe a little of both." I pause, shoving my hands into my pockets as I search for the right words. "Actually . . . I am grappling with something."

Father nods, and I sense he already knows what I want to say. He doesn't prod, just watches me, giving me room to speak.

"It's about a girl, Daisy," I finally admit.

"Ah! I thought as much. A girl."

"And my duties."

He raises an eyebrow, encouraging me to continue, so I take a seat beside him.

I tell him about Daisy Walker, starting with our first meeting. I tell him about our adventures through Porto, about falling in love with her, staying in touch for a while, and then ending it abruptly. Because I thought it was the right thing to do.

"But Father, my heart is pulling me toward Paris, toward Daisy and the possibility of her being the one for me. My forever princess. But my mind—my royal training—reminds me of the inescapable truth. You are ill. And the kingdom needs a king. And a king needs a queen. And Mother says Daisy, an American girl, is not suitable."

Father places a steady hand on my shoulder. "Leo, the greatest disservice you can do to those you love is to live half-heartedly, bound by hesitation. If you believe Daisy is part of your future, you must go to her."

He gazes out at the rose garden, his face reflective. "Knowing one's time is limited changes everything. It sharpens what's truly important. And you, my son, need to understand that love isn't a burden to be hidden or cast aside."

I stare at the ground, absorbing his words. "But what about Daisy? I thought staying away was protecting her, sparing her from the chaos of this life. But maybe . . . I've only made things worse. I want to see her again, to tell her everything. But if I leave for Paris, it feels as if I'm leaving everyone here in limbo. And with you . . . ."

Father grows more serious, his gaze intense. "Leo, go to Paris, speak to Daisy. Find the answers you're looking for." He looks at me with an intensity that penetrates to my core. "Leo, when you take the throne, you must do so without regrets. You must have a heart that's full, not divided."

I swallow, nodding as I feel the truth in his words. "Thank you, Father. You've helped me more than you know."

As I stand, his voice softens. "I want to see you and Leif both happy, Leo. I want you to live lives you can be proud of, and to love someone with your whole heart. So go, speak with her, live fully." He pauses, his voice growing even softer. "And know that I am always proud of you."

I nod, feeling that fierce determination settling within me. "I will, Father. I'll do everything I can."

"You should. You have almost three months until the ball. After that, it's out of your hands."

The sun disappears and stars pop out glittering up the dark sky. I leave my father's side, more certain than ever.

First, I have to find James. Then, Olivia. Then figure out how to find Daisy and tell her everything so that she'll fall in love with me before the Christmas Ball.

Kingdom of Arandel

Chapter Sixteen

LEO

Later, I sit on the edge of my bed, my elbows resting on my knees, staring blankly at the ornate tapestries on the wall opposite me.

My room, one of the most lavish in the castle, feels suffocating tonight making it impossible to focus on anything except the clock that seems to be ticking louder in my head.

Three months. Three months to figure out if Daisy Walker is my future or just a dream.

My mind drifts back to Portugal, to the golden beaches and the smell of salt in the air.

I can still feel the warmth on my skin and hear the waves crashing against the shore as I paddled out into the Atlantic Ocean for some of the best waves in Europe.

I remember riding a wave back in and seeing Daisy sitting on the sand with her sister, her eyes wide as she spotted me walking toward her.

My beautiful girl jumped up and ran over to me, full of questions about how it felt to ride a wave.

I wanted to pick her up and kiss her right then and there. But the idea that she was leaving soon to go back to Maine and that I would be continuing my travels to Asia and Africa stopped me.

We only had those few weeks, and I didn't want to spoil them by making it a vacation fling.

I couldn't stop my hand from brushing away the springy curls that floated into her eyes, though.

I hadn't meant to do that, but my hand burned to do it again. And again. I wanted desperately to wrap a hand in her hair and drag her lips to mine.

Feel her gorgeous curves in my arms.

The church bells clang loudly, snapping me out of my daydream. It's morning already. I have not slept a wink.

"Daisy, my love, I am coming to find you."

I scroll through social media, looking for recent posts that might give me an idea of where she lives in Paris.

If I have to wait outside the Sorbonne for her to enter or exit, I will.

The Sorbonne!

I have friends there. My *brother* is going there! Oh my God! Suppose she runs into Leif?

We are identical twins. Most people can't tell us apart physically, but once they get to know us, it's easy.

I hadn't told her who I was. How could I? At the time, I'd been desperate for an escape from my royal life, from the expectations that came with being Prince Leopold of Arandel.

I didn't want her to see me as anything other than the boy I was pretending to be—just Leo, a guy on a gap year before college, a guy who loved the ocean and was in no rush to figure out his future.

And Daisy, well, she didn't care about titles or royal bloodlines. She cared about books and writing and flowers—lots of flowers.

We were living life in the moment.

Now, the moment is frozen in time.

Mother's words echo in my mind. "She's an American girl. Not brought up to be a Queen."

The image of Daisy in a royal court, wearing a crown, standing beside me as Queen feels so distant, so impossible. But the alternative—marrying someone else, someone chosen for me—feels like a prison.

Three months to figure it all out. To discover if Daisy can love me the way love her.

As my eyes close down, I feel my hand reaching for Daisy's smooth brown one.

"You are my Queen, Daisy Walker. You and only you."

Chapter Seventeen

DAISY

Friday night comes faster than I expected. Between all our preparations and shopping for a new dress for me, Lulu and I are exhausted by the time we turn on the twinkly lights surrounding our rooftop paradise.

Lulu's got a lot more skills than dressing dolls, that's for sure.

She's done an amazing job. She's bouncing between guests, making sure everyone has champagne, laughing with our neighbors, and teasing me like always.

I tug at the hem of my mint green mini-dress, feeling both bold and a little out of place. Lulu insisted I wear it, saying it's the perfect balance of cute and sexy for a Parisian balcony party.

I have to admit, it does feel good. The dress flutters lightly in the breeze, and I catch sight of my reflection in the window—rosy cheeks, wild curls, and a grin that refuses to disappear.

Tonight is perfect.

Jake, our hunky cowboy neighbor, stands beside me, his southern accent so different that people admire him whenever he says anything at all.

"This is some party y'all got here, Daisy. Ain't nothing like this back in Alabama."

I laugh, taking a sip of champagne. "Thanks. It's all Lulu. I'm just along for the ride."

"Well, you sure are somethin' to look at tonight," he says, warmly.

I stifle a giggle. "You sure are too. Lulu adores your cowboy hat."

"I don't leave home without it."

Something about his easy charm makes me relax, and I'm glad he agreed to come tonight.

But I can't help gazing around the crowd.

It's ridiculous, really. I shouldn't be thinking about Étienne. Or maybe I should? After all, I invited him, and he's been on my mind since our first class together. There's just something about him—quiet, mysterious, and that intensity in his eyes when he sketches. . . .

"Daisy, darling!" Lulu's voice breaks through my thoughts as she drapes an arm over my shoulders. "Why do you look so serious? You've got quite the crowd of admirers tonight. I'm jealous!"

She winks at Jake before turning her attention to the rest of the party. "Isn't this great? Everyone's having fun, and look at you, surrounded by all these men!"

I laugh, shaking my head. "Oh, stop. It's not like that."

"Sure, sure," she teases, glancing over to where Maxine, my new friend from the Sorbonne, is chatting animatedly with some other classmates. "Maxine looks like she's in heaven. And what about your handsome artist? Have you spotted him yet?"

"Not yet," I admit, trying to keep my voice light. "But he said he'd come."

Lulu grins, her eyes sparkling mischievously. "Oh, Étienne better watch out. You're looking too good tonight. Even Jake here has some competition."

I roll my eyes at her, though my heart flutters at the thought of Étienne showing up.

But just as I'm about to scan the crowd again, something—or rather, someone—catches my eye.

And everything around me freezes.

The air leaves my lungs as my eyes lock onto a figure standing at the balcony's edge talking to some well-dressed men.

It can't be. But it is.

Leo.

My breath catches, and my heart pounds wildly in my chest. He's standing right there, looking at me like . . . like he's never seen me before.

For a split second, the world tilts on its axis. All the emotions I thought I'd buried—the confusion, the heartache, the longing—they come rushing back, crashing over me like a wave.

He's here. After months of silence, after ghosting me and disappearing without a trace . . . he's here, at my party.

But something's wrong. He's just staring at me with a neutral look like I'm a stranger.

Before I can move, before I can process what's happening, he turns abruptly and walks away, disappearing into the crowd.

"Leo?" I whisper, my voice barely audible. I feel frozen, rooted to the spot, as I watch him leave, unable to understand what I've just seen.

Lulu is still next to me but she's oblivious to what's just happened.

Jake says something I don't catch, his voice muffled by the fog of confusion in my mind. I don't respond. I can't. My whole body feels numb.

I've been dreaming of seeing Leo again for months. Fantasizing about what I'd say if we ever met again, how I'd demand answers, make him explain why he disappeared.

But now that he's here—was here—I'm speechless. I didn't even have the chance to say his name before he was gone. Again.

It's like the universe is playing some cruel joke on me.

"Daisy, you okay?" Lulu's voice cuts through the haze, her hand on my arm, steadying me. "You look like you've seen a ghost."

I blink, trying to pull myself back to the present, but my heart is racing, and the party feels too loud, too overwhelming. "I . . . I think I need a minute."

Without waiting for her response, I push past the guests, making my way through the apartment, my mind spinning. I have to get out of here, away from the crowd, away from the questions swirling in my head.

I stumble into the small bathroom and close the door behind me, leaning against it as I try to catch my breath.

What just happened?

Was that really Leo?

He looked just like him, but something was off.

The way he looked at me . . . as if he had no idea who I was.

I run my hands through my hair, trying to calm the panic rising in my chest.

Leo is in Paris. He came to my party. But why did he leave? Why didn't he say anything?

And why did he look at me like that?

As I stand there, staring at my reflection in the mirror, a thought begins forming in my mind. A terrible, confusing thought.

Did I *imagine* him?

Am I so nuts about that boy that I imagined he was at my party?

Chapter Eighteen

DAISY

I splash cold water on my face, forcing myself to breathe. Whatever just happened with Leo—or whoever that was—I can't let it ruin the night. Not now. Not when the party is going so well.

With a deep breath, I leave the bathroom and make my way back to the balcony, determined to push the strange encounter out of my mind.

I'm here to have fun, and that's exactly what I'm going to do. I spot Maxine in the corner, laughing with a few classmates, and head straight for her.

"Hey, where've you been?" Maxine asks with a grin, her eyes sparkling under the twinkle lights.

I shrug, trying to play it cool. "Just needed a minute. You know, all this champagne can catch up to you."

Maxine snickers. "Girl, tell me about it. The French take 'wine with every meal' very seriously."

I laugh, grateful for the distraction. Maxine clinks her glass against mine. "Here's to your amazing fête."

I'm still laughing when I catch sight of Étienne stepping onto the balcony, looking as effortlessly stunning as ever.

He's no Leo.

He's definitely real, and he's definitely here.

Etienne is dressed in a casual button-down, his dark hair falling into his eyes. He wears his intensity like a shield.

"Daisy?" Maxine nudges me, noticing my attention wandering. "Oh, I see what's going on here."

I blush. "What? No. I just . . . I invited him. It's not a big deal."

"Sure, sure," she teases, but I don't have time to respond because Étienne is walking toward us. I clear my throat, trying to shake the weird mix of nerves and excitement bubbling inside me.

"Étienne, you made it," I say, flashing him a smile.

Lulu appears at my side instantly, her grin wide and mischievous. "Oh, the artist! Daisy's been talking about you."

"This is my roommate, Lulu." I feel my cheeks burn.

Étienne, with that cool, calm demeanor of his, just gives a small nod, his gaze flickering over to me before settling back on Lulu.

"Nice to meet you."

Lulu, ever the life of the party, winks at me. "Nice to meet you, too. Now, Daisy, I'll leave you to introduce Étienne to the rest of your admirers." She waggles her eyebrows before bouncing off to chat with someone else.

I groan internally. "She's . . . a lot."

Étienne's lips twitch in a small smile, but those piercing eyes of his lock onto mine, and suddenly I wish I was sitting down. The intensity in his gaze makes my heart race in a way that's so different from the light, easy vibe I get with Jake.

Jake, who's now calling my name from across the balcony, holding up two champagne glasses.

"Daisy, come on! Let's dance before I drink all this without you!"

"Duty calls," I tell Étienne, and head over to where Jake is waiting, the music shifting to a lively hip-hop beat.

I can't help but laugh as Jake spins me into the dance, his energy infectious and light.

We move to the beat, his goofy moves making me laugh until my sides ache. Jake is easy to be around—no pressure, no intensity, just fun.

But every time I glance toward Étienne, it's like being pulled into a different world.

When the song ends, I find myself catching my breath and making my way back to Étienne.

"You're not much of a dancer, huh?" I ask, teasing a little.

Étienne shakes his head. "I prefer to watch."

"So, what's your latest project? Still sketching strangers in the lecture hall?" The champagne has me speaking freely and a bit brashly.

Étienne's voice is low and serious. "I've been working on something different. More abstract, less . . . structured."

"Abstract, huh?" I lean in, intrigued. "I'd love to see it sometime."

Gosh, can I be more obvious? Am I throwing myself at him? And why? So I don't start feeling sad and rejected by Leo all over again?

Etienne meets my gaze. As if he understands there's more going on here than simple questions about his art.

"Maybe," he says, his voice quiet. "Maybe I'll show you."

The moment stretches between us, and for the first time tonight, I'm completely lost in the magic of the evening.

The lights, the music, the buzz of champagne—everything feels surreal, like a dream I don't want to wake up from.

By the time the party winds down, I find myself leaning against the balcony railing, the twinkle lights above me casting a soft glow.

Étienne has gone, and Jake is chatting with some other guests.

I take a deep breath, feeling the cool night air on my skin, and for the first time all night, I let myself think about Leo. Just for a moment.

He's in Paris. Or . . . was.

Maybe it wasn't him after all. I still don't understand what happened earlier, but I do know one thing: I can't keep wasting my energy on someone who walked out of my life without a word.

Tonight, with the champagne fizzing through my veins and the laughter of my friends echoing around me, I decide that this is the last time.

The last time I'll let Leo take up space in my mind.

I'm done chasing ghosts.

Hopefully, this particular ghost is done with chasing me too.

Chapter Nineteen

LEO

I lean back in my plane seat. Only three more hours before the royal jet lands at Orly, and we can head to the family's apartment in Paris.

I was surprised to learn that Leif isn't staying there. When Mother told me he's living with a college friend to get the whole university experience, I felt a tiny stab of envy.

Leif doesn't have to *pretend* to be a regular guy. Yes, he's a Prince, too, but not the Crown Prince. He can do whatever he wants to . . . to a certain extent.

He can marry whomever he wants or even, not marry if he doesn't choose to. It's completely up to him.

The last time we spoke, Leif made it clear that he wanted to live a life far from mine. I understood his frustration at always being "second" or the "spare" heir, but it wasn't my fault.

Sometimes, I feel as if Leif despises me. James is more my brother than Leif. He understands the pressure of being the heir. But he doesn't have a twin to deal with.

“Are you ruminating again?” James asks, tossing the pillow at me. “You know it makes you ugly. Daisy won’t like it.”

Just hearing her name makes my heart feel like it’s going to fly out the window.

“Dude, I can’t believe I’ll be seeing her again.” I cover my face with my hands. “I hope she won’t be mad I ghosted her for the past few months. I hope she’ll let me explain and forgive me.”

“That’s a lot of hoping you’re doing, brother. I say you buy her a nice, expensive gift. She’ll forgive you.”

“Nah, man, Daisy isn’t like that. And besides, she doesn’t know who I am. I can’t show up with a diamond necklace and say, ‘Here you go.’ She thinks I’m a poor student on a gap year. I was working as a waiter when she met me.”

James hoots. “I heard there are some openings at a Paris restaurant. You want me to make a call? You can get another job.”

I roll my eyes at my buddy. “You’re a pest.”

“And you’re a mess. A royal one.”

“Tell me about it,” I groan. “Now help or shut up.”

Kingdom of Arandel

The jet circles the sparkling lights of Paris as we prepare to land. I make a silent promise. I’ll do whatever it takes. Not just for me, but for Daisy. I’ll make her happy. I’ll love her like no one else can.

The plane banks hard, and it jolts me out of my thoughts.

“Welcome back to reality, Prince Leopold,” I mutter.

"Why can't you just call her and tell her you're on your way?" James asks, buckling his seatbelt.

"I can't contact her," I gripe. "I promised."

James raises his perfectly trimmed eyebrows. "Who did you promise? Her book boyfriends?"

He wipes his face with a hot cloth a flight attendant passes to us on a tray.

"If you must know, I promised her sister, Corrine. She introduced me and Daisy in Porto. I spent a lot of time with them, so Corrine got to know me well. We all went to Paris together for a few days, too."

James frowns. "I don't get it. Why would you make such a dumb promise?"

"It's a long story."

I never told James that I stopped talking to Daisy because I thought it was best for her. For us both.

Our lives were on two different continents. Our time zones were six hours apart. But most of all, I didn't think our paths would cross again. Once I returned to Arandel to assume my duties, I wouldn't be able to travel freely and hang out with her. I didn't know how to tell her we had no future. At least that's what I was thinking months ago, before I realized I couldn't live without her.

"Do we need drinks for this story?" James asks.

"No."

"Well, tell me."

I rub my eyes and sigh. But I tell James everything. "She didn't agree with me, smart girl. But when she tried calling me, I didn't pick up. I thought I was being strong for us both."

"Jerk," James says.

"I was a jerk. I was being stubborn. I really thought I was doing the right thing for Daisy."

"Don't ever do the right thing for me please."

"Ha! I won't for anyone. Who the heck am I to decide what's right for someone?"

"You learn quick, little grasshopper."

"Anyway, Corrine called. I tried to tell her that a long-distance romance with no end game was not benefitting me or Daisy. Corrine called me a terrible person and made me promise to never talk to Daisy again. Since then . . . well, I've been a total mess, as you can see. I've been sick about this. And I can't contact her because Corrine said I would deeply regret it."

"Whoa! Does she know you're the future King of Arandel?"

I shake my head. "No. Neither does Daisy."

"All of that you've been keeping inside?"

"Yes," I say miserably. "How could I mess up this badly?" I close my eyes. "I really like her, dude."

James sits in silence.

When the plane's wheels touch down, he turns to me and says, "We ride at dawn."

"Not funny."

He raises his eyebrows. "I'm not kidding."

I do my best to ignore him. This is not a joke. My life is on the line here. Well, my heart is, but it's essentially the same thing.

As we walk through the airport to our car, James asks questions about Daisy. He says he's gathering intel.

"Since we can't call her, we have to figure out a way to meet her organically."

"Well, she goes to the Sorbonne, that's all I know."

"Suppose she has another boyfriend?" James says, his tone light, like he's not worried. But his words hit like a brick.

I glare at him. "Don't say that."

He shrugs. "You should be prepared for anything."

"I'm not prepared for that."

"May the best man win, then." James grins, but there's something serious beneath it.

I frown. "Are you trying to make me more nervous?"

"Nope. But I brought my spears in case."

I groan. "I'm not fighting anyone."

James leans in, his expression softening. "Look, we didn't come all the way to Paris, negotiate a three-month reprieve with your family, just for you to leave empty-handed. You're getting the girl, Leo."

Moments like this is why James is next in line to lead the Zulu Nation. He makes decisions, sticks to them, and doesn't waste time overthinking things.

I'm the opposite. Like Shakespeare's Prince Hamlet, I ruminate over every scenario, every possibility.

I look at James. "How about I show her how I feel and see if she reciprocates? I'll do my best."

James smirks. "Good thing I can have five wives if I want. Less pressure."

"Not helping."

He chuckles. "Sorry."

The thought of ending up without Daisy—of her walking away—terrifies me. But I only want her to be mine if she loves me back. That's the thing. She knows the side of me that surfs, who worked at that café in Porto, who danced with her under the stars at a reggae concert.

But would she want the other part of me too? Can she love the prince as well as the surfer?

If she can love even half of me, that'll be enough because anything less would break me.

Chapter Twenty

DAISY

Every morning, Paris greets me with its soft golden light. I walk along the cobblestone streets, past the boulangeries, where the scent of fresh croissants fills the air.

My favorite part of the walk comes when I reach the Pont des Arts. There's something about this bridge—covered in locks, each one representing a promise, a story, or a dream—that pulls at my heart every time.

The Seine glistens below me, reflecting the early morning sun.

Boats glide along the water, their wake creating soft ripples. I stop at the same spot every day, right by a cluster of locks I've come to think of as "mine."

I don't know these couples, but there are a few locks I always check on, as if their stories are somehow tied to mine.

There's one in particular that always catches my eye: "Amélie & Julien, 15 Juin 2006." It's been here for fifteen years, weathered and worn but still holding strong. I wonder what happened to them. Did their love last? Or did it fade with time, like the rusty metal of the lock?

As I trace the letters with my fingertips, I hear footsteps approaching.

I turn to see a familiar face—the young city worker I met weeks ago, the one who told me about the locks. He's wearing his bright orange vest again, carrying a clipboard under his arm.

"Bonjour, mademoiselle," he says, with a quirky smile.

"Bonjour," I reply, smiling back. "We meet again."

"Seems like we're both creatures of habit," he chuckles. "How's your morning walk?"

"It's my favorite part of the day," I admit, glancing back at the locks. "But I'm worried about them."

"That's actually why I'm here. I wanted to tell you—the city made a decision."

"What kind of decision?"

He sighs. "They're removing all the locks. Starting next week."

My heart sinks. "All of them?"

He gestures to the bridge's railing. "The weight of the locks is causing structural damage. They have to be removed for safety reasons."

I stare at the locks, the thousands of little symbols of love. "That's . . . so sad."

"I know," he says softly. "I thought you'd want to know."

I nod, still trying to process the news. But then an idea hits me. "Is there any way I could . . . keep some of them?"

He raises an eyebrow. "You want to keep the locks?"

"Just a few," I explain quickly. "There are a couple that seem . . . special. I want to try to find the people who left them. Maybe they'd like their locks back."

I hope he doesn't think I'm nuts. "What else will you do with them?" I ask.

He looks at me thoughtfully, then smiles. "That's a sweet idea."

"I just hate the thought of them being destroyed," I continue, feeling a little more hopeful now. "I'd like to return them to their owners. If they want them."

He extends his hand. "I'm Marc, by the way. I'm happy to help you do that."

I shake his hand. "Daisy. Nice to officially meet you."

"Likewise," he says with a grin. "Tell you what—if you come back on Friday morning, I'll make sure you get the locks you want. You can show me which ones, and I'll set them aside for you."

I brighten instantly. "Really? That would be amazing!"

He chuckles. "I think I can arrange it. You've got until then to decide."

"Thank you so much, Marc. Seriously." Then another idea pops into my head. "Actually, I'm going to try to track down more owners before then, and see if they want their locks."

Marc looks intrigued. "How are you going to do that?"

I bite my lip, thinking it through. "Social media, maybe? Some of these locks have names and dates on them. I could post photos and see if anyone recognizes them."

His smile widens. "You're really committed to this, huh?"

I laugh, a little shy. "I believe in love stories."

"And you're trying to save them," he says, his voice warm with admiration. "You're quite the romantic, Daisy."

I shrug. "I've heard that more than I can count."

We stand in comfortable silence for a moment, watching the river as it flows beneath us. The Eiffel Tower peeks out in the distance, standing tall against the brightening sky.

"I should get going," he says, glancing at his watch. "But I'll see you Friday?"

"Friday," I agree with a smile. "Thank you again, Marc."

He gives a small bow, a playful glint in his eye. "*À bientôt*, Daisy."

"*À bientôt,*" I reply, watching as he walks away, weaving through the few early pedestrians.

I look down at the names etched into the metal, each one representing a love story that mattered to someone.

I snap a few photos on my phone, starting with Amélie & Julien's lock. Then "Sophie + Lucas, 12 Mai 2010" and "Emma & Thomas, 21 Août 2015."

I have three days to try to find them, and I'm determined to do it.

As I walk away from the bridge, my heart feels a little lighter. I don't know if I can save these locks, but I'm going to try. And maybe, just maybe, this will help me feel better about losing Leo.

Later that evening, I sit at our tiny kitchen table, my laptop open and a cup of tea steaming beside me. Lulu breezes in, dropping her bag by the door.

"You're home early," she remarks, peering over my shoulder. "What are you up to?"

"Trying to save love," I say with a wry smile.

She raises an eyebrow. "Ambitious. Tell me more."

I explain the situation—the locks being removed and my plan to find the couples.

"That's so you," she says fondly. "Always the romantic."

"That's what I keep hearing. Maybe it's silly, but I feel like I have to do something."

"It's not silly at all." She places a hand on my shoulder. "Do you need help?"

"Actually, yes." I brighten up. "I was going to post these photos online, see if anyone recognizes them. But your French is way better than mine. Could you help me write the posts?"

"Consider it done." She pulls up a chair. "Let's craft the most heartwarming messages Paris has ever seen."

Together, we compose heartfelt posts in both English and

French, sharing the photos and explaining the situation. We tag local groups, use popular hashtags, and ask others to share.

"Now, we wait," Lulu says, hitting 'post' on the last one.

I lean back, a mix of hope and anxiety fluttering in my chest. "This will work, I feel it."

As the night wears on, we chat and laugh, the conversation drifting to lighter topics. Like the dolls she dressed. The paintings I saw in class.

As Lulu is getting ready for bed, washing her face, and doing all kinds of pre-bed rituals I'd never think of like slathering moisturizer on my eyebrows, she suddenly stops.

She swings around in a flourish, arms on her hips.

"Missy, you were the belle of the ball. Just like I predicted."

"What?"

"I forgot to tell you."

"What?" I ask again, my eyes scanning the social media posts for any Likes or comments.

"Someone asked for you today."

"Who?"

"*Il est tres beau.*"

"Every guy is very handsome to you," I giggle.

"No, my dear," Lulu strikes a hand on her heart. "He is . . . *superbe* . . . but kind of a snob."

"Ugh!"

"Yes, I told him you were taken."

I gasp at my friend. "I'm not taken."

"Not yet."

"What's his name? What does he look like? Maybe I will remember him from the party."

"Leif Montclair."

"Oh, never heard of him. He isn't in any of my classes."

"But he goes to your school. He came with a bunch of other snobs from the Sorbonne."

Lulu teases me that I attend a rich, snobby university.

"Well, next time, get his number for me. Aren't you always saying I need to go out more?"

"Yes! But with darlings like our neighbor, the gunslinger, Jake. Or that sexy troubled artiste, Étienne. Not this haughty, I'm-too-sexy-for-my-shirt, Leif Montclair."

"Gunslinger Jake," I giggle. "I'll have to tell him that one."

Lulu chuckles. "Have you seen the way he walks? Like he's ready to pull out two pistols at the drop of a hat."

"Lulu, stop. Jake is a Philosophy major. He *thinks* for a living."

"He can think about me *anytime*," she retorts.

I end up laughing all the way to my bedroom. One thing about living with Lulu, there's never a dull moment.

I climb into bed, still scrolling through the posts we made earlier.

In the back of my mind, I can't shake the feeling that this mission is about more than just the locks. It's about believing in love, in connections that stand the test of time.

And maybe, just maybe, it's about finding the courage to let go of the past and open myself up to new possibilities.

With Jake the Gunslinger. Or moody Étienne. Or even this new guy, Leif Montclair. Who knows?

Chapter Twenty-One

LEO

I don't have time to waste. Less than three months to get Daisy back. To make her fall in love with me again. Or maybe for the first time. I'm not even sure where we stand, but I know one thing: I can't lose her.

I stand in front of the mirror in the gym, absently adjusting my form as I push through another set of weights. James's next to me, huffing dramatically between reps, though I'm pretty sure he's more interested in offering advice than actually working out.

"So, remind me again," James says, pausing mid-lift. "You're trying to find a girl who thinks you're just some broke student on a gap year?"

I grunt in response, wiping sweat from my brow. "Exactly."

"And all you know is that she goes to the Sorbonne?" James raises an eyebrow, clearly unimpressed. "You didn't think to get, like, any more details? An address? A last name maybe?"

"I have her last name," I mutter. "Walker. Not exactly narrowing things down."

James lowers the weights with a sigh. "Man, this is like searching for a note in a song."

I don't answer him. Instead, I grab my phone, scrolling through Daisy's social media, looking for some clue, some hint of where she might be in this massive city.

The usual posts flood her feed—pictures of Paris, random art sketches, quotes about love. But none of it helps. I know she's at the Sorbonne, but beyond that . . . nothing.

James catches me staring at my phone. "You're stalking her social media again, aren't you?"

I roll my eyes. "I'm looking for clues."

"Dude," James laughs, shaking his head. "You sound like a detective in a bad movie. What's the plan? You just gonna show up at the Sorbonne every day and hope you bump into her?"

"I don't know," I admit, frustration creeping into my voice. "I can't waste time, James. If I don't find her soon . . . ."

"If you don't find her soon, what?" James sets down his weights and grabs a towel, smirking. "You're gonna disappear forever? You're the Crown Prince of Arandel. I think you'll survive."

"It's not about me surviving," I snap. "It's about her. I . . . I need her to know the truth."

"What truth? That you're going to be a King?" James nods as if this makes perfect sense.

"No. That I love her. Daisy's not going to care if I'm a King or a commoner. I mean, not in reality. Maybe in theory. She believes in fairytale romances, true love . . . all that stuff. It's who she is."

James grimaces, pretending to gag. "True love? Fairy tales? Man, you really are in deep."

I'm about to respond when my phone vibrates in my hand. I glance down, and my heart skips a beat when I see a new post from Daisy. It's a picture of the Pont des Arts, the bridge covered in locks, with the caption: *Trying to find these couples so I can return their locks. Love deserves to be saved.*

Something clicks in my brain.

"I've got an idea," I mutter, mostly to myself.

James raises an eyebrow. "Oh no, you've got that look again. What are you thinking?"

"She's trying to find the couples who put their locks on the Pont des Arts," I explain, showing him the post. "What if I . . . pose as one of them?"

James looks at me like I've lost my mind. "Pose as one of them? You mean, pretend you're part of some couple who locked their love on the bridge?"

I nod, feeling a glimmer of hope. "Exactly. If she's looking for them, I can reach out. Send her a message to start the conversation. It's a way to get her attention."

James smirks, crossing his arms. "So, your grand plan is to lie to the girl you want to fall in love with?"

"It's not a lie," I say quickly. "Not really. It's a . . . it's a way to connect with her. I'll figure the rest out later."

James shakes his head, laughing under his breath. "I don't recommend it."

"The sooner I find her, the better for everyone."

James leans back against the wall, crossing his arms. "Well, then. Looks like you've got a new mission. Better get to it, Romeo."

I nod, pulling up Daisy's post again, my mind racing. If I can find the right words, the right way to reach out . . . maybe this crazy idea will work.

Chapter Twenty-Two

DAISY

The sun is just starting to set as I sit on the balcony, my phone propped up in front of me. My sisters' faces pop onto the screen, all five of us filling the frame. It's our weekly catch-up session—The Alphabet Sisters pow wow. No matter where we are in the world, we make time for this.

"Hey!" Ava waves from her gelateria in Portland, Maine. Her hair's pulled back into a messy bun, and I can already see her trademark, sprinkle-covered apron. "Okay, so you guys have to hear about this new flavor I've been working on. Chocolate hazelnut with a dash of sea salt. I'm calling it Salty Sweet Surprise."

"Girl, I'm booking a flight just for that," Bridget says, leaning back in her chair. Behind her, the olive trees wave their feathery branches. "But what's this 'surprise' about?"

Ava grins mischievously. "Oh, something extra I'm working on with Tyler."

Corrine, who's in Porto, raises an eyebrow. "Extra? Like what? Are we talking about gelato or . . . something more?"

We all laugh, and Ava blushes, biting her lip. "Okay, fine, fine. I might've meant that Tyler and I are, you know, talking about the future . . . maybe taking the next step."

Bridget practically cackles. "What step, Ava? Are we talking rings? Babies? A vacation home in Italy? Spill!"

Ava waves her hand, looking flustered. "It's nothing serious—yet. We're just talking."

"Talking, huh?" Corrine teases, grinning as she adjusts her screen to show Salvador, her very attractive European fiancé, cooking in the background. "Talking always leads to something serious."

Ava laughs, but there's that look in her eyes—the one that says something *is* happening, even if she's not ready to admit it yet. I smile at the screen, loving how no matter what, we always tease each other but with love behind it all.

"What about you, Corrine?" I ask, shifting the attention away from Ava. "How's your master's degree going?"

"Oh, it's great! I'm buried in translations, but it's fascinating. Salvador's helping me with the tougher stuff. I swear, his brain is as sexy as the rest of him." She winks at me, and I laugh. Salvador waves from the kitchen, oblivious to our conversation.

Bridget takes a sip of wine, her eyes twinkling. "And what about Emerald? Miss Climate Warrior. How's the fight going?"

Emerald, who's been mostly quiet, speaks up. "I'm working on a major offshore wind project, as you all know. It's huge, guys. It's a real step toward renewable energy independence."

"Wow," Bridget says, impressed. "That sounds amazing."

Emerald shrugs, her expression all business. "It's important. This planet isn't going to save itself."

Then she turns to me, a mischievous grin forming. "But enough about wind turbines. Daisy, have you been kissed yet?"

I groan internally, sinking into my chair. "Really, Emerald?"

She crosses her arms. "I'm just saying! You're in Paris—the city of love! And you're still the only one of us who hasn't been kissed."

Bridget raises her glass. "She's right, you know. You need to get out there, Daisy. Meet someone. You're *Daisy Walker*, for crying out loud! You should have men lining up for you."

I open my mouth to protest, but Corrine chimes in. "Don't be so shy, sis. You've always been the romantic one. Just find someone who makes you laugh. Someone who makes you feel special."

I hesitate, thinking about Jake and Étienne. Should I tell them? It feels weird to bring it up, especially after what happened, but I force myself to say something.

"Actually, there's this guy," I start, hoping I sound casual. "Jake. He lives in my building."

"Ooh, tell us more!" Ava leans in closer to the screen, her eyes wide with curiosity.

"Well, he's . . . he's really sweet. Friendly. Southern accent. We've hung out a couple of times." I try to sound like it's more than it is, like it's something significant, but deep down, I know it's not.

"Sounds promising," Corrine says. "I want you to enjoy yourself, Daisy. Don't feel like you have to date."

"Of course, she has to date," Emerald argues.

"Yeah, well . . . he's just a neighbor." My enthusiasm fades, and the conversation moves on, but I can't shake the hollow feeling. I glance down at my phone, half-expecting someone to mention Leo.

Bridget blurts it out, laughing. "Remember when Daisy was all about that—"

"Shh!" Ava hisses, cutting her off.

I look away from the screen for a second, my heart tightening at the mention of his name. The teasing continues, but I feel disconnected, like I'm floating outside the conversation. They don't know. They don't know how hard it's been, not knowing where Leo is, why he disappeared, or why he showed up again just to vanish.

But I force myself to shake it off. "Jake's . . . great," I say, trying to bring back the focus.

I see the flicker of approval in their eyes, but even I can hear the lie in my voice. I know my sisters can too. After we say our goodbyes and hang up, I sit back in my chair, staring out at the Eiffel Tower in the distance.

I lied. Again. I tried to make it sound like I'm falling for someone else, like Leo doesn't still have a hold on me. But who am I kidding?

"Fairy tales don't just happen," I mutter to myself, watching the lights of Paris start to twinkle as the sun sets.

I have to remember what Emerald told me before I left home. *You have to make your own fairy tale.*

But how? How do I do that?

I sigh and lean back in my chair, letting the breeze wash over me. Maybe I need to stop waiting for something magical to happen and start creating it myself.

An idea flits through my mind—something simple, but bold. I could ask Étienne out. He's quiet, sure, but there's something about him that intrigues me. Or maybe I'll spend more time with Jake, see if there's something more between us.

I don't know yet, but I do know one thing: I can't wait around anymore. If I want my fairy tale, I'll have to make the first move.

Chapter Twenty-Three

DAISY

I spot Étienne just outside the Sorbonne, leaning casually against a low wall with his sketchbook tucked under his arm, as usual.

There's that quiet, almost mysterious air about him. I take a deep breath, trying to calm the nervous energy bubbling inside me. I'm going to ask him out, I think.

It's Paris. Why not?

I smooth my dress, gather my courage, and walk over. "Hey, Étienne."

He looks up, his dark eyes locking onto mine. "Hey, Daisy."

I fumble with my words for a second, then blurt it out. "I was wondering if you'd like to get coffee with me sometime?"

Étienne raises an eyebrow, that mysterious smile widening slightly. "Why not right now?"

I blink, caught off guard. "Right now?"

He shrugs, pushing off the wall with an effortless grace. "Sure. There's a café just around the corner."

I can't help but laugh nervously. "Okay, yeah. Right now sounds good."

We walk together through the narrow streets, the rhythm of Paris surrounding us.

The sounds of people chatting, the smell of fresh croissants, and the soft sunlight filtering through the trees make everything feel like a scene from a movie.

I glance at Étienne as we walk, trying to calm my racing heart. He's so different from Leo. Where Leo is all golden warmth—his white-blond hair catching the light—Étienne is darker, more intense.

We reach the café, a charming little place with round tables spilling out onto the sidewalk.

The chairs are painted bright colors, and tiny flowerpots decorate each table. It's so perfect, so Parisian, that I almost pinch myself.

We sit down, and I catch a glimpse of my reflection in the café window.

My dark curls, my flowery dress—I feel like I've stepped into a different world. A world where I'm the main character in a book, about to have a romantic adventure. It feels . . . surreal.

We order our coffees, and I try to make conversation, but Étienne's gaze is intense. It's like he's studying me, seeing past the words I'm saying.

"Can I ask you something?" Étienne says after a few moments.

"Sure," I reply, trying to sound casual, though his attention is making me self-conscious.

"I've wanted to sketch you since the first moment I saw you," he says, his voice quiet but steady.

I stare at him, shocked. "What?"

Étienne leans back in his chair, his dark eyes never leaving mine. "There's something about you. An inexplicable quality about you."

I blink, trying to wrap my head around what he's saying. "Inexplicable?"

He nods slowly, studying me like I'm already one of his sketches. "It's like you have an innocence, but at the same time . . . depth. That pulls people in."

I laugh nervously, feeling my cheeks burn. "Yeah, it's called innocence," I say wryly.

Étienne's lips curve into a knowing smile. "Maybe. But I would be honored if you would sit for me. Let me sketch you."

The idea of him sketching me feels strange, intimate even. But there's something thrilling about it too. "You want me to . . . pose for you?"

"If you'd be comfortable with it. I know it sounds a bit weird. I promise it isn't. Or, it won't be. We can do it at the park sometime."

"Okay," I say, a little breathless. "Yeah, let's do it."

Étienne's smile widens, and before I say another word, he pulls out his sketchbook and flips to a fresh page. "What about now?" he says, reaching for his pencil. "I can start now."

"Right now?" I ask, startled again. I'm frozen for a second, not sure what to do or how to sit.

But Étienne looks so focused, so calm, that I just take a deep breath and settle into my chair. The café around us fades into the background as he begins to sketch, his pencil moving fluidly across the paper.

"You can talk while I draw," he says quietly, not looking up from the page.

I don't know what to say at first, so I just start talking about the usual—Paris, classes, the bridge with the locks. But somehow, the more his pencil moves, the more I start to open up.

I tell him about my sisters, about growing up in Portland, Maine. And then, before I realize what I'm doing, I start talking about my mom.

"I was seven when she passed," I say softly, my voice trembling slightly. "She had cancer."

Étienne doesn't say anything, but his gaze is so intense, so focused, that I keep going. "I was the second youngest. My sisters were devastated. I . . . I did my best to be strong for them. I guess I thought if I could be tough, it wouldn't hurt so much."

I pause, staring down at my hands. "But it did hurt. I just . . . didn't let myself show it."

The memory of those years, of losing her, feels like it's pressing down on me. My voice cracks, and before I know it, tears are sliding down my cheeks. I wipe at them quickly, embarrassed.

Étienne stops sketching and looks up at me. Without a word, he reaches across the table and gently wipes a tear from my cheek. The gesture is so tender, so unexpected, that I'm caught off guard.

"I didn't mean to make you cry," he says in despair.

"I don't . . . usually talk about her," I whisper. "I guess being in Paris, being on my own, it's bringing things up that I've kept buried for a long time."

"Sometimes it takes being seen to finally let yourself feel."

His words settle over me like a warm blanket, and for a moment, we sit there in silence, the sounds of Paris swirling around us. I've never opened up like this, not even to my sisters. But something about being here, with Étienne, feels different. Like it's safe to let the cracks show.

"You get that, don't you?" I ask, looking at him closely for the first time. "It's like you understand something deeper. What's your story, Étienne? You don't talk much about yourself."

Étienne leans back, his pencil still hovering over the page. He hesitates, his dark eyes flickering with something I can't quite read. "I suppose I don't."

"So, tell me," I press gently. "What are *you* hiding?"

He lets out a small laugh, though there's no humor in it. "I'm not hiding anything. But I am . . . carrying things. Like you."

I lean in, waiting.

Étienne sighs, setting his pencil down for a moment. "I grew up here in Paris. My mother was an artist, just like me. My father left when I was young, so it was just the two of us. She used to take me to all the museums, the galleries. She'd always tell me that art was the one thing that could capture the truth without needing words."

He pauses, his gaze drifting over the people walking by. "She passed away last year."

I feel my chest tighten. "I'm so sorry, Étienne."

He shakes his head softly. "It's alright. She lived for her art, and she died doing what she loved. But it changed me. I can't look at the world the same way anymore. I used to see beauty everywhere, but now . . . now I feel like I'm always chasing shadows."

There's a heaviness in his voice that I recognize. It's the weight of grief, the kind that never really goes away.

"I guess we're both carrying things," I say quietly, my heart aching for him.

"Maybe that's why I wanted to sketch you. You remind me of what I lost but also of what I'm trying to find again."

I stare at him, speechless, feeling a deep connection I hadn't expected.

"Would you sit for me at the park tomorrow?" Étienne asks, his voice gentle.

I nod slowly. "I'd love to."

It's then that I realize, Etienne is all about his art. It will always come first for him.

He smiles, picking up his pencil again. "But for now, let me finish this sketch. I'm almost done."

See!

I watch him as he starts sketching once more, the café fading into the background as he captures something in me I didn't even know was there. And for the first time in a long while, I feel like maybe I'm not carrying this burden alone.

Chapter Twenty-Four

LEO

I'm sitting in the back of the limo, the leather seat cool beneath me, but my nerves are burning.

Outside, students are pouring out of the Sorbonne, laughing, chatting, heading to wherever their next class or coffee date is. I'm watching them like a hawk, waiting. Hoping to see her and approach her. Nice and simple.

James's in the front, his feet propped up on the console, scrolling through his phone. Every now and then, he glances at me with that knowing look.

"So, you're really doing this, huh?" he says, not looking up. "Operation Say Hello to Daisy is Plan B?"

"Maybe," I mutter, my eyes fixed on the entrance. "I've been rethinking the first plan."

"Rethinking Plan A?" James snorts. "Man, you were all set to pretend you were some couple from a decade ago just to get her attention. What's the change of heart?"

I run a hand through my hair, frustrated. "It feels wrong. Like a trick. Maybe I should try to see her . . . the normal way."

James raises an eyebrow. "Hence, Plan B. But stalking her campus in a limo? Real subtle, Leo."

I ignore his sarcasm, shifting in my seat as the door to the Sorbonne swings open. Then I see her.

Daisy.

She's walking out of the building, her dark curls catching the light, her flowery dress swirling around her legs. She's more beautiful than I remember.

The sight of her makes my chest tighten painfully. I've imagined seeing her again so many times, but nothing could've prepared me for this.

She looks . . . radiant. Like the city itself has shaped her into something even more stunning.

"There she is," I whisper, more to myself than to James.

James leans forward, peering out the window. "Damn. She's even more gorgeous than you said."

I can't respond. My throat feels tight, and I can't tear my eyes away from her. But then I see him.

The guy she's staring at.

A tall, lanky French guy. Dark tousled hair and wounded eyes, like he's waiting for the world to crack open and swallow him. The kind of guy I'd buy a beer for and listen to him talk. Just not this time.

"Whoa!" James's feet hit the mat. "Incoming."

He's walking right beside her now. His dark curls blow about in the breeze and whip into his eyes.

"Ouch! He's got that sexy Frenchman look down, dude. Might be stiff competition."

"Hush!"

"Just saying. He looks like he stepped out of some artsy black-and-white film. Very . . . what's that English word . . . ah, yes, '*broody*.' A lot of women love that type."

My heart hitches in my throat. James is right. I hope that's not her type, though. I pray under my breath they're just friends.

Daisy smiles at something he says, and I feel a sharp sting of jealousy. I can't look away.

They stop outside the gates, and she's talking to him, her smile lighting up her whole face.

There's nothing in her demeanor that says she misses me at all. I might as well be a ghost.

"You gonna follow them?" James asks his attention fully on me.

I hesitate, torn between the impulse to run after her and the nagging thought that maybe . . . maybe she's happy. And I'd be interfering.

"I don't know," I mutter.

Before I can make up my mind, James turns to the driver. "Let's get moving, man."

The limo starts to roll forward slowly, and I catch one last glance of Daisy and the guy. They're walking toward a café nearby, the kind with little round tables and chairs on the sidewalk.

It's the kind of place Daisy loves. I know because she and I sat in cafés like this one, talking for hours in Porto and in Paris.

My heart just got kicked in the ribs.

We watch as they slide into seats.

James whistles low. "So, this is the guy, huh? Mr. Sketchbook? What's his deal? You think he's using the old 'let me sketch you' line?"

My jaw clenches as I watch the guy pull out his sketchbook and start drawing her right there at the café.

"Is that . . . normal?" I ask my voice tight. "Isn't that a little . . . weird?"

James shrugs. "I mean, some artists are into that kind of thing. But yeah, I'd say it's a bit of a move. You know, romantic, intimate . . . she's probably all flattered, thinking she's his muse or something."

I grit my teeth as I watch Mr. Dark and Broody's hand glide across the paper.

Daisy's expression changes from smiles and flowers to something I've never seen. She looks so . . . vulnerable. She's talking, and as she speaks, I can see her getting upset.

I watch her, her hands fluttering in her lap, and then it happens.

She starts crying.

And the artist—he—reaches out and wipes her tears away. My blood boils.

"That should be me," I mutter, gripping the seat so hard my knuckles turn white. "That should be me."

James looks at me. "What do you want me to do? Cause I'm ready. We can swoop in right now."

I shake my head. "That would push her away. She's not a damsel in distress. My Daisy is strong."

But knowing Daisy can handle herself doesn't mean I'm okay.

I feel like I'm suffocating. Watching them together feels like a knife to the heart.

What have I done?

I walked away from her, from this, to chase some ridiculous idea of freedom, to surf and pretend like the world wasn't waiting for me to grow up. And now I'm watching her slip away, right in front of me.

"I've been such a fool," I say quietly, staring at her. "I thought I wanted freedom, but Daisy . . . she's everything. She's so much more than that."

James gives me a long look. "You're in love with her?"

I swallow hard, my chest tight. "Yeah. I am."

It hurts to admit it, but I'm in love with her. I've been in love with her since the moment I met her, and I've spent months running from it. And now . . . now I don't even know if I should interfere.

"She looks happy, doesn't she?" I ask James, my voice low.

James squints at the café. "I don't know, man. She was crying like two seconds ago. But look, this dude's definitely in her space. You sure you want to let that happen?"

I lean back, my mind spinning. Is it fair to show up now, after all this time? After I disappeared from her life without a word? What if she's happy? What if this sensitive French artist is what she needs?

Do I have the right to interrupt that?

But then I remember the way she smiled at me. The way she laughed when we were together. I felt like I could be myself around her—like I wasn't just the Crown Prince, the guy with all the responsibilities weighing him down.

With Daisy, I was just Leo.

I take a deep breath, clenching my fists. "I'm going back to Plan A. I'll email her," I say suddenly.

James raises an eyebrow. "What happened to 'the normal way'?"

"I'll reach out to her first, let *her* find *me*."

James sighs, shaking his head. "Man, you're playing a dangerous game. But okay. Let's head back to the apartment, then."

"No," I say, sitting up. "First, we're going to the Pont des Arts."

James's eyes widen in disbelief. "The bridge? You're serious?"

I reach into my jacket and pull out the lock I bought yesterday.

"Where'd you find a pink lock with hearts in one day?"

I turn it over, and James lets out a low whistle. "It has a daisy, too? How?"

"It's Paris; they sell these romantic locks everywhere. You can have anything engraved on them. That's a cool thing about Paris. You can literally lock yourself to the city."

James guffaws.

I twirl it, feeling the cool metal against my skin. It's small, but I've had it engraved on one side with *Leo loves Daisy*. On the other is a daisy and a word meant just for her.

James lets out a low whistle. "You know you're supposed to do that with the person you love, right?"

I give him a small smile. "I know. But I'm doing it anyway. Even if she never sees it, I want it there. And imagine if she finds it."

James shakes his head, grinning. "Plan C! Now I see how you won our Strategic Studies course award. Me, personally, I think you should call her. Or let me call her. Forget that promise to her sister. But hey, love makes people do crazy things, right?"

I nod. "Yeah. It does."

The driver pulls away from the café, and I sit back, the lock still in my hand, my heart racing with the knowledge that I will keep devising plans until Daisy and I are back together again.

Chapter Twenty-Five

DAISY

Lulu and I weave through the bustling marketplace, the late evening air filled with the scents of fresh herbs, roasted nuts, and warm bread.

The stalls are lively, vendors shouting out deals, their tables piled high with fruits, vegetables, cheeses, and handmade trinkets. Paris always feels alive, but tonight, there's an extra energy buzzing around us.

I hold up a bunch of lavender, inhaling its calming scent, but my thoughts are anything but calm. "So . . . I had coffee with Étienne."

Lulu perks up, turning her attention from the stall she's been browsing.

"Wait, hold up. *The* Étienne? Mr. Dark and Mysterious? And I'm just now hearing about this?"

I laugh, shrugging as I tuck the lavender into our shopping basket. "It wasn't a date. I mean, I don't know if he thinks it was."

Lulu raises an eyebrow, clearly unimpressed with my nonchalant tone. "Daisy, come on. Coffee in Paris with a guy like that? Sounds like a date to me."

"*Well* . . . ," I start, unsure how to describe the mix of emotions still swirling inside me. "It was nice. He's . . . intense. But not in a bad way. We talked, and he sketched me."

Lulu stops in her tracks, her eyes wide. "*He sketched you?* That's straight out of a romance novel!"

I blush, feeling the heat rise to my cheeks. "Yeah. I mean, it was . . . surreal. Like, the whole café scene was so perfect I kept waiting for someone to yell 'cut' like we were in a movie."

Lulu sighs dramatically, nudging me with her elbow. "I swear, you are living the dream. Sitting in a cute Parisian café with a hot artist sketching your beautiful face? Ugh. Some of us have all the luck."

I laugh, but then something flickers in the back of my mind—*Leo.*

"I did feel something weird, though," I admit, my voice quieter.

Lulu tilts her head. "Weird, how?"

I glance around the market, trying to find the right words. "It's going to sound crazy, but . . . I swear I felt Leo's presence."

Lulu frowns, her playful expression fading. "Leo? As in the one who disappeared?"

"Yeah." I run a hand through my hair, feeling silly for even bringing it up.

"I know it sounds ridiculous. He's probably not even in Paris. But there was this moment—while I was sitting there with Étienne, talking about my mom—I swear I caught a whiff of his scent. It's a lemony smell he always had? Like he washed his hair with lemon trees or something."

Lulu's eyes widen. She gives me a long look. "You think he's back?"

"I don't know," I say, shaking my head. "I was so caught up in everything that I didn't have time to focus. But for a split second, it felt like he was nearby, watching or something. I could've been imagining it, though."

Lulu crosses her arms, a thoughtful look on her face. "Maybe it's your subconscious playing tricks on you. I mean, you haven't let go of him, have you? Not really?"

I sigh, looking down at the produce stall in front of us, my fingers brushing over the fresh tomatoes. "No. I haven't."

Lulu doesn't say anything. She just gives me a sympathetic nudge. We move along the market, but that nagging feeling won't leave me alone.

And it's not just the coffee date. I stop for a moment, chewing on my lip as I think about the party we threw on the balcony a few nights ago.

"You remember the party?" I ask.

"Of course," Lulu says. "It was *epic.*"

"Well, I thought I saw him there too. Leo," I admit, my voice barely above a whisper.

Lulu's eyes widen. "You never mentioned that."

"I didn't want to sound crazy," I say, shaking my head as I think about it. "But there was this moment when I saw a guy who looked exactly like him. I mean, it *was* him. I'm sure of it. He was just . . . standing there, staring at me like he didn't even recognize me. And then he was gone."

Lulu lets out a low whistle. "So he's haunting you now?"

"That's what it feels like," I say, my voice small. "Like he's everywhere. I keep thinking I'm over him, that I'm ready to move on, but every time I take a step forward, he's right there. Like some ghost I can't shake."

Lulu looks at me, her face softening. "Maybe that's because you haven't had closure, Dais. You never got to say goodbye."

I don't respond, because she's right. I never got that closure. Leo just vanished, leaving me to piece together the fragments of whatever we had. And now, I'm stuck somewhere between letting go and still holding on.

Chapter Twenty-Six

DAISY

We continue exploring the fantastic outdoor market. It seems that vendors from all around the outskirts of Paris come here once per week to sell their wares. The freshest fruits, vegetables, mushrooms, chocolate, honey, and more. I can't get enough of the choices.

"On to a new topic," I say.

"Please." Lulu strokes an avocado.

"I got a message about the locks."

Lulu's eyes light up. "Ooh, tell me!"

I pull out my phone, scrolling through the message I received earlier.

"It's from a woman who saw my new IG account, *Locked in Love.*"

Lulu hoots. "That's so you, Dais."

"She said she and her beloved locked it there over fifteen years ago, and she wanted to know if it was still there. A large red lock with their names, *Melanie and Trevor forever.*"

"That's so sweet!" Lulu beams, leaning in to read the message over my shoulder. "Look at you, reuniting lovers with their tokens of romance."

I grin. "I'm so excited! I'm going back to the Pont des Arts tomorrow to check. If their lock is still there, I can help them get it back."

Lulu gives me a little hip bump as we continue walking. "You're such a hopeless romantic, Dais. Look at you. Saving love."

I think about how Leo and I helped save my sister Corrine's love with Salvador Torres. It had been my mission, and Leo joined in with no question.

I wish I could have saved our love. But it was out of my hands.

"I don't know," I say, smiling to squash the memory. "It feels like the right thing to do, you know? These locks mean something to people. If I can help them get them back . . . I'm doing something good."

Lulu sighs happily. "You *are* doing something good. You get to be Cupid. Imagine *that* on your resume."

I chuckle, tucking my phone back into my bag. "If I'm Cupid, I'll need some arrows." I glance around the market. "Where's the arrows?"

We pass a vendor selling fresh flowers. Lulu grabs a bouquet of peonies and hands them to me. "You don't need arrows. Flowers are your weapon of choice."

I nod. "They are. Thank you."

I could imagine my sister Emerald rolling her eyes at how cliché Lulu and I are together.

I place them carefully in our basket.

Lulu smiles, looping her arm through mine. "You're going to find the lock. And help a lot of couples. And hopefully . . . ," she stops.

"Hopefully what?"

She looks at me with utter seriousness. "Will you find some time for Étienne, too? I mean, he's real. He's here. And he's not going anywhere like you-know-who."

I blink. "True. I like him. He makes me feel . . . ," I almost say "*seen*," but I end with "special."

"And don't forget Jake."

"I won't. He asked me to go on a walking tour this weekend. Of our neighborhood."

Lulu grabs three tangerines and juggles the bright orange fruit. "Watch this."

I laugh as she tosses the three round objects higher and higher into the air. She spins around and keeps up the performance.

"Wow!" I breathe. "You're good at this."

"So are you," she winks. "Just not with tangerines."

A loud snorting laugh escapes my mouth. "You're horrible, Lulu."

"Me!" she exclaims in mock shock. "I'm the one trying to keep up with your shenanigans. Two real men and a ghost man."

"You forgot one."

Lulu drops the fruit into our basket. "I did?"

I bite my bottom lip as I admit to something I've suspected. "I think Marc may like me."

"Marc? Who the hell is Marc?" Lulu rolls her eyes. "Give me the basket before I need to toss another tangerine in it."

I laugh again. "He's the city worker giving me the locks they cut off the bridge. He's the one who started this project with me. I told you about him."

"The plot thickens."

"There's no plot. He's nice."

"And he has a job, so that's something, right? Étienne is a poor, starving artist. Jake is a philosopher, so you know what that means . . . poor and penniless again! And the ghost of Leo has no pockets."

"You're ridiculous, Lulu. Let's go home."

"Not before we grab some cheese for tonight. Should we get goat? Sheep? Or one that goes well with champagne?"

I stop in my tracks. "We have champagne?" I peer into the basket.

We arrive at a table filled with a multitude of fancy-looking bottles.

"Voila! Pick one. This is champagne direct from France's Champagne region, which, by the way, is not far from Paris."

"We can't afford this?" I whisper out the side of my mouth.

Lulu shakes her head. "In France, the champagne is not as pricey as outside France. Choose, just not the Dom Perignon."

I eye the labels. "They all look very pricey to me. Let's wait until we have something to celebrate," I say.

Lulu picks up a bottle. She hands over some euros and puts it in our basket.

"Live like a French person, Daisy. Where champagne is concerned, every day is a celebration."

I doubt that is true, but I don't argue.

"We will be the penniless ones," I scoff. "If we *live* like a French person."

Lulu chuckles. "I got so lucky this year with you, Dais."

I smile. "I got lucky with you, you mean. And I like my nick-name, Dais."

"You should know I mean, '*d a z e.*'"

"Daze?"

"Because life with you is a whirlwind of fun."

"No one's ever said that about me before. Emerald says I don't live enough."

"That was before Paris. BP."

"Yes, BP."

As we walk through the bustling market, my thoughts drift back to the bridge and the locks.

Why do I keep being drawn back there? What do the locks mean for me?

And what's up with this woo-woo feeling that Leo isn't as far away as I thought?

Chapter Twenty-Seven

LEO

James insists we stop for champagne.

Not just any champagne, of course.

No, he's got the driver pulling up in front of a fancy shop on Rue de Rivoli, the kind of place that sells bottles wrapped in gold foil with price tags that make your head spin.

"Dom Pérignon," he says with a grin as he climbs back into the limo, clutching the bottle like it's a prize. "Did you know that Dom Pérignon was a monk? A monk! Lived his whole life with nothing to do with women. Isn't it ironic that his champagne is the drink of choice for people celebrating love?"

I laugh, shaking my head. "You have the strangest facts, man."

James pops the cork, the sound crisp and satisfying, and pours the champagne into two paper cups we had lying around. He hands one to me with a mock toast. "To monks and the pursuit of happiness."

I smirk, lifting my cup. "To Daisy."

We sip, the bubbles hitting me harder than I expected. Dom Pérignon is no joke. By the time we're back in the limo, driving toward the Pont des Arts bridge, I'm already feeling a little lightheaded. The city lights blur together as we ride along the river, and I find myself laughing at everything James says.

"I'm just saying," James chuckles, taking another sip from his cup. "It's funny, right? This guy makes the greatest champagne ever, and he's got nothing to celebrate with. No wife, no girlfriend. Just bubbles."

I grin, the champagne fizzing through me, making everything seem lighter, easier. "Well, here's to Dom. I'll drink to that."

We clink our paper cups together again, and James tips his head back, laughing. The driver circles the bridge a few times, looking for parking, and by the time we finally get out of the car, we're both a little tipsy.

I stumble slightly as we make our way to the bridge, James holding onto my arm like a protective big brother. "Easy there, Romeo," he says, smirking. "We still have a lock to place."

The weight of the small lock presses into my palm, a reminder of why I'm here. I'm not just drunk and laughing with my best friend—I'm about to lock something to this bridge that I hope will get Daisy's attention. I hope it'll make her remember me, think of me.

We reach the railing, and I take a deep breath. The lights from the river dance across the water, and everything feels... right, somehow. This city, this moment.

James stands beside me, looking out at the view. "So, you gonna do it?"

I nod, pulling the lock from my pocket. It's silly and romantic and maybe even a little desperate, but it feels right.

"Okay," I say, my fingers trembling a little as I snap the lock onto the bridge. The sound clicks into place, and for a second, it feels like something's shifted in the universe. I swallow hard. "I want to say a few words."

James rolls his eyes but smiles, crossing his arms. "Oh boy, here we go. Let's hear it, Prince Charming."

I clear my throat, trying to gather my thoughts. "Daisy . . . you are the most amazing person I've ever met. I was a fool to walk away. I'm locking this here because . . . I want you to know that I'm here now. I'm not running anymore. And I'm not giving up on us."

James nods, his grin fading slightly as he listens. For a moment, everything feels still, like the world is holding its breath.

When I finish, James claps me on the back, pulling me into a quick hug. "Not bad, man. Not bad at all."

We both laugh, the weight of the moment dissolving into a light, bubbly feeling—probably thanks to the Dom Pérignon still buzzing through our veins.

I take another sip from my cup, looking down at the key in my hand. "What do I do with this?" I ask, holding it up. "You're supposed to throw it in the river, right?"

James frowns, shaking his head. "You wanna contribute to more pollution, dude? Think of the fish. They don't need a bunch of keys floating around in their water."

I blink, realizing he's right. "Good point."

He smirks, taking another sip. "You could always swallow it. Keeps it safe forever, right?"

I choke on my drink, laughing. "I'm not swallowing the key, James."

"Come on," he teases. "It's romantic! You swallow it, then you have the lock in your heart forever."

Before I can respond, a man in a bright orange vest approaches us, clipboard in hand. I recognize him as one of the city workers. He's clearly finishing up for the day, his steps slow, casual.

He stops when he sees us locking the lock and smiles warmly. "Congratulations, gentlemen," he says, nodding at the lock. "You've made your love official."

James nearly spits out his champagne. "Whoa, whoa, whoa. We're not—" He waves his hands around, laughing. "No, man, we're not together. We're just . . . locking something for someone else."

The worker looks between us, eyebrows raised. "Oh?"

I rub the back of my neck, feeling the heat rise to my face. "Yeah, it's . . . it's for a girl. Her name's Daisy. She's been looking for locks on this bridge. I wanted her to see this one. It's mine. It's for her."

Marc's face softens, and he steps closer, peering at the lock. "Daisy, huh? I know her. Sweet girl. She comes here every morning, checking for the locks."

My heart skips a beat. "You know Daisy?"

He nods, smiling. "Yeah, she's been trying to reunite some couples with their locks. I think it's her little project."

James's eyes widen, and before I can stop him, he pulls out a wad of cash and holds it out. "Alright, buddy. Here's the deal. You make sure Daisy sees that lock. Read it. Make it a whole moment for her, okay?"

Marc waves away the money. "My name is Marc." He looks at us skeptically. "Does she know you?"

James pushes me forward. "Yes. She knows him."

I'm dying to say, "She's my future wife," but that may sound creepy. He'd never show Daisy the lock.

Before I can say a word, Marc speaks up. "I'll be honest with you. I like her more and more every time I talk to her. I was thinking of asking her out."

I groan, covering my face. "Great. More competition."

James snickers, patting me on the back. "Yeah, well, not even your title stands a chance against good ol' Paris charm. You've got your work cut out for you."

"She's worth it."

James waves the billfold in my face. "I could pay him *not* to ask her out."

I shake my head.

To Marc, I say, “I’m sorry. Please don’t mind us. We’re leaving. I apologize for my friend’s rudeness.”

James sucks his teeth. “You’d never last a minute in the wild.”

I push James toward the end of the bridge, where our car is waiting for us. “We’re in *Paris.*”

“Where the lion gets eaten by the mouse.”

“Good luck, gentlemen,” Marc says.

“Thanks,” I say, hurrying off, praying the guy doesn’t decide to clip my lock and toss it in the trash.

Back in the limo, James goes over our options. Number one is staking out the bridge in the morning.

When I don’t respond, James asks. “Well?”

I pat his shoulder. “Glad I have you as my comrade. Afraid for anyone going up against you.”

He snorts. “Got that right. But seriously.”

I feel a strange mix of hope and anxiety bubbling up inside me. The lock is in place. The message is clear. Now all I can do is wait and hope that Daisy sees it—and understands what it means.

James takes another sip of champagne, nudging me. “Well, Romeo, it’s done. Now what?”

I stare at the water as we drive alongside the riverbank, the lights reflecting off the river. “Now . . . we wait.”

Chapter Twenty-Eight

DAISY

The early sunshine filters through the lace curtains in my room, casting a soft golden light on my face.

I stretch, yawning, and reach for my phone on the nightstand. First things first—check my IG page, *Locked in Love*.

I sit up quickly when I see the notifications: five new messages. I swipe through them, my heart skipping with excitement.

One from Russia, one from Greece, and three from the United States, all about locks they left on the Pont des Arts bridge years ago.

I grin, opening the first message. It's from a woman in Moscow.

Hi Daisy, my boyfriend and I locked a small silver lock on the Pont des Arts in 2012. We wrote our initials, N&M, on the front, and we attached it near the middle of the bridge. Do you think it's still there?

I scroll to the next one, and my excitement grows.

Hey, Daisy. My wife and I visited Paris for our honeymoon in 2010. We locked our love there, right under one of the lamps, and we're still going strong. If you find a red lock with "G+S 4ever," it's ours.

The stories go on. Each makes my heart race a little faster, the sheer *romance* of it all washing over me.

There's a message from a man in Scotland who rode his bicycle through Paris, fell in love, placed a lock on the bridge, and kept riding out of town. Does he deserve to find his true love after he disappeared like that?

Yes! My inner voice shouts. They all deserve to find their true love, even you. Especially you.

Hush! I scowl. "This is not about me."

I scroll past Mr. McFadden's message and move it to my folder of possible locks to locate. His description of the lock is too vague. I'll have to message him back and ask for more details.

My little project is taking off. It's more than I ever imagined. People want to find their locks. They want to reconnect with their love stories. I'm not the only hopeful romantic out there.

I can't wait to tell my sisters. They always think of me as too much in the clouds, all dreamy and unrealistic.

But now, I feel validation. As if there's a reason I've believed in fairy tales for so long.

Look how excited people are about finding their love locks. Who would have thought?

Well, duh, me.

I sit up fully, brushing a hand through my curls as I read through each message again, smiling to myself. Their descriptions—initials, colors, years—I can't wait to see if I can find them.

I glance at the clock. It's early, the perfect time to get to the bridge before the tourists flood the area. I type up a quick post for my page:

Excited to see so many of you sharing your love stories! If I can't find your lock, don't worry! Tell me your story, and we'll make this page a virtual bridge—a place to celebrate love, forever.

Within minutes, Likes and hearts pour in. My heart beats faster as a new plan hatches.

I'm so excited I fall out of bed, my feet tangling in the covers.

Geez, Daisy, get a grip.

I pull on a long, swirly skirt and a sweater. Despite the sunshine, it's fall in Paris, and a bit chilly.

I hurry down the stairs of our building and run right into Jake. He's coming in the door with a bag holding a long, fragrant baguette and a cup of coffee.

I inhale the bread and look wistfully at the coffee.

"You want to share?" he offers.

"I would love to, but not today. I've got to get to the Pont des Arts bridge before class."

"Is this about your *Locked in Love* IG? Lulu told me about it."

I nod, almost drooling over his baguette. I swear these French know their bread.

"Yup."

"Okay, I'll follow you."

"It's about love," I warn him. "I know you're like a profound thinker doing a Master's on French philosophers."

"And . . . ? Ya'll think philosophers know nothing about love. Darling, we know the most."

Jake's Southern accent could rattle anyone. It certainly sends shivers up my spine.

I press my lips together so I don't end up drooling over the baguette *and* Jake.

"Okay, follow me, please. I'd love to hear your thoughts on love." I gather my skirt to sweep out the door of our building.

In his Southern drawl, he says, "I was thinkin' 'bout a fun way we could explore Paris this Saturday if you're still up for it."

I stop in my tracks. "Yes. How?" I could listen to Jake's accent all day.

"We're gonna *ride* 'round Paris. Don't ask how. It's a surprise."

Images of tall, broad-shouldered horses flit through my mind.

"You said you like romance," he smiles.

"I do. Just . . . ."

"What?"

"I've never ridden a horse."

Jake's laugh is so loud it probably wakes Lulu on the fourth floor. "Darlin', we ain't riding horses."

"Oh, okay," I slump a little bit.

Am I disappointed? Yes!

I imagined riding around Paris on the back of a horse with this tall, sexy cowboy-looking man. I swear, the love stories are going to my head.

Chapter Twenty-Nine

DAISY

On my walk to the bridge, my head buzzes with all the exciting things happening.

I have a Saturday adventure with Jake to look forward to.

Étienne and I are meeting in the Luxembourg Gardens after class this week so he can sketch me amongst real flowers.

Maxine and I are starting a romance book club with some other students and choosing our first book this week.

And there's always that guy Leif Montclair, who goes to my University. The one Lulu says is a snob. His number is still sitting on my desk.

Back home in Maine, I didn't have a boyfriend or dates. But here in Paris, it's as if the possibilities are endless.

What's different? I heard travel expands your horizons.

Living in Paris has more than expanded my horizons; it has created a brand new one—one filled with boys.

I imagine all the lovers and dreamers who've walked these streets—F. Scott Fitzgerald and Zelda, their laughter echoing along the Seine, their footsteps brushing the same stones under my feet.

Will I be one of the people falling in love in Paris? One day?

A thrill goes through me at the idea that Ernest Hemingway himself may have rested his arms on the bridge and looked down at the river.

Or Van Gogh.

Vincent Van Gogh must have strolled along this riverbank, noticing the yellow leaves dripping off the trees when the breeze swirled around them.

And Picasso. I squint at the Cathedral of Notre Dame up ahead. Did he wander along here, too? Maybe discussing art with a student? Or one of his lovers?

I want to twirl around on the bridge. I'm so excited to be a part of Paris's creations.

The buildings along the river stand like silent witnesses to all the love stories that flourished in this city. And hopefully to one of my own, too.

THERE ARE HARDLY ANY TOURISTS, SO I GET STARTED searching amongst the locks.

I snap photos, trying to capture the colors and the names etched into the locks. Maybe someone will recognize their own.

I scan the bridge, looking for the specific descriptions from my messages.

A red lock with initials near the center.

A silver one by a lamp post.

But there are hundreds, no, thousands of locks here. It's overwhelming.

I hear footsteps approaching as I crouch down to get a closer shot.

"Morning, Daisy," Marc's familiar voice calls out.

I turn as he approaches. "Morning, Marc. Tell me you're not cutting them off today."

"Not yet. But soon. I bought you a little time."

"Really? Thanks. I'm getting messages from people interested in getting their love locks back. Even couples who are no longer together. It's evidence of their once true love."

Marc stands beside me, leaning against the railing. "Any luck finding the ones they're asking for?"

I shake my head. "Not yet, but it's early. I'm still hopeful."

He glances at the rows of locks lining the bridge, his expression softening.

"You know, I've been working on this bridge for almost two years now. It's funny how these little pieces of metal hold so much meaning for people."

"Yeah," I agree, turning to face the river. "Each one tells a story."

"Right," Marc says, nodding thoughtfully. "It's kind of like how the bridge itself tells a story. You know this bridge was originally built in the early 1800s? But it was destroyed during World War II. The one we're standing on now was rebuilt in the 1980s."

I look at him in surprise. "I didn't know that."

"Yeah," he continues, "I'm studying architecture, so I geek out over this kind of stuff. The Pont des Arts has been through a lot—kind of like the couples who put their locks here. Surviving through time, weathering storms, but still standing."

I smile at that idea. "You're a romantic too, Marc."

"I'm French. I live in Paris, the city known for love. It's part of our DNA."

I grin. "I bet. I feel different here myself."

"How so?"

I don't want to admit to him that I feel beautiful in France. I duck my head to hide a tell-tale redness creeping across my face.

"You're a soufflé, bubbling over with passion, Daisy; anyone can see it. You don't need to hide from it."

"What?" I can't believe this man who hardly knows me says I am a bubbling soufflé of passion. I haven't even kissed anyone yet.

Marc's eyes soften. "Just an observation. Excuse me if I stepped on any lines. The French step on all the lines. Haven't you heard?"

I smother a little laugh. "You blame everything on being French, huh?"

"Of course," he sweeps an arm outward. "Look at what French passion does. Almost breaks a bridge with all these added metal symbols of it."

I grow solemn. Marc has a point. Love can make you do things in the moment that you may later regret or that have consequences you never dreamed of.

"I just wish someone loved me enough to want to put his name on a lock with mine and throw away the key."

Marc looks at me for a moment, then says softly, "Maybe someone has."

I laugh lightly, but I hear the wistful edge to it. "I wish," I try to joke. "But no one loves me like that. Not a forever kind of love."

Not yet, I think.

Marc pauses, his eyes steady as he studies me. "I think you're wrong."

I blink, surprised by the certainty in his voice. "What do you mean?"

He shrugs, but there's something in how he looks away, as if he's hiding something. But what could Marc be hiding? He barely knows me.

"I don't know. I just think . . . you deserve that kind of love. And maybe it's closer than you think."

His words hang between us, charged with a meaning I can't quite grasp. I smile softly, touched but unsure how to respond.

"Thanks, Marc."

He clears his throat to change the subject.

"Hey, maybe we could visit other bridges one Saturday when I'm off. I could give you their history. There are plenty of bridges besides this one, you know."

I grin, glancing around at the locks with a fondness that fills my chest. "But this one is my favorite!"

He chuckles. "Of course, it is. What was I thinking? You're as devoted to this bridge as all the couples who stood here before you."

I laugh, feeling more comfortable now. "Exactly."

He gestures to the locks with his clipboard. "Let me know if you need help finding any of those. I'll be around."

I nod. "I will. Good luck with your architecture studies, by the way. That's impressive."

Marc grins, his usual carefree confidence slipping back into place. "Thanks. I'm hoping you'll be standing on a bridge I've designed one day."

"I look forward to it."

He gives me a final nod before walking away. I watch him go, his words still swirling in my mind.

Did someone put a lock on this bridge with my name on it?

Chapter Thirty

LEO

I lean against the railing of the private houseboat James rented close to the Pont des Arts bridge.

James suggested it was a way for him to relax and drink champagne while we put Plan C into action, which is me waiting for Daisy to find my lock.

When she finds it, I will get off this boat and run to her to explain how much I miss her and how sorry I am to have disappeared from her life.

But now that we're on board the houseboat, with servers bringing buckets of champagne and oysters on the half shell, I realize how crazy it is. How would I get past all these people unless I dive into the Seine?

Plan A, for me to impersonate someone looking for his locked love is equally hopeless. So far, no response. Not to mention Plan B, stalking her at the Sorbonne is illegal *and* impractical.

None of these genius plans are working.

"We need a Plan D," I mutter.

"I agree, it seems impossible for your little pink lock to stand out amongst all those others."

From this viewpoint, I see what he means. The sun reflects off the locks as if they're a wall of metal, blinding me.

My eyes dart to Daisy every time she stops to look at a lock, hoping, praying, she'll find mine. But nothing yet.

It's Saturday morning. I figured she'd be at the locks for most of the day. But no such luck.

After a couple of hours of lock hunting and lots of photos, including some with random tourists who I think are asking about her lock project, Daisy leaves.

I watch as she puts away her notebook and phone, swings her backpack on her back, and, poof, disappears amongst the tourists.

My heart was jumping up and down when I could see her.

But now that she's gone, it has plunged to my toes.

How can one person have such a dramatic effect on me?

James stands beside me, sipping his champagne. He's being too calm for my liking.

"We should have bribed Marc," he says. "This would be over."

"She'll never find it, will she?"

He doesn't look hopeful. "How is Plan A going? Did you send her the messages?"

"Yes, I am Grumpy McFadden from Scotland looking for my wee lass who I met twenty years ago in Paris while riding my bike along the canal routes of Europe."

James nods appreciatively. "That sounds like something we should do. For real."

"Right?"

"And?"

I shrug. "No response. Maybe she's gotten too many messages and hasn't read mine yet."

James smacks my back. "Have you used the "Do you want to be a real-life princess" card?"

I shrug off his hand. "I told you Daisy wouldn't care about that."

James shakes his head. "If you want to connect with Daisy, you need to throw everything to the wall. And your royal card is the first thing I'd pitch to any wall. Because it'll stick."

I rub the back of my neck. "I sent her private *and* public messages on her *Locked in Love* account. Told her how great this whole project is for people worldwide."

James raises an eyebrow. "And?"

"And . . . nothing." I shrug, trying to sound nonchalant. "She hasn't written back."

James gives me a sideways look. "The royal card, trust me."

I sigh. "I was hoping she'd respond . . . just something small. At least to know she's seen it. I need to reconnect with her as just Leo. Not as the Crown Prince of Arandel." I scrub my face with one hand.

It hasn't helped that in my morning videochat with Mother, she was surprised I hadn't talked to Daisy yet.

Her exact words were, "You can't cook a meal if you don't put it on the fire first, Leo."

"Ewww, Mother. Daisy is not a meal. And what do you know about cooking?"

"Touché," Mother said. "Touché." It was a rare smile from Mother, but at least she smiled.

James watches me for a beat, then nudges my shoulder. "Come on. Let's do something to get our minds off this. Polo at Bagatelle?"

I glance up. "Polo?"

He nods. "Yeah, Polo de Paris. We can clear our heads. Besides, there's nothing like knocking some sense into each other with mallets."

I laugh despite myself. "Yeah, fine. Let's go."

Kingdom of Arandel

Chapter Thirty-One

LEO

The car drives us to the Polo de Paris club on the riverbanks of the Seine. The polo grounds at Bois de Boulogne are sprawling, framed by tall trees that line the riverbanks of the Seine.

Horses with gleaming coats graze near the manicured lawns. The tension in my chest loosens when I see the horses flicking their ears and tails.

James and I suit up, grab mallets, then head out to the field. It doesn't feel right to be playing when Father is sick and I've still not connected with Daisy, but James says we need a fresh outlook.

So here we are.

The Montclairs of Arandel have been members of this polo club for over a century. Not a bragging right, just a fact. I'm grateful they can accommodate us at the last minute.

One day, I'll take Daisy on a horse ride all over Paris. I bet she'd love that.

"Daydreaming of your princess?" James asks, pulling on boots.

"Yeah, I want to take her on horseback all around the city."

"I'd do that."

"Find your own princess and it's a double date," I joke, but I mean it.

I can't imagine a better way to live than with people I love. My girl and my best friend.

"Here comes your brother," James interrupts my lofty thoughts.

A fire poker hits my stomach.

I stand with feet apart as if ready for battle.

Leif approaches, leading a tall, sleek black stallion. The horse's coat shines like polished onyx, its muscles rippling with every step. Leif's hand grips the reins confidently as he walks up, his movements as controlled and precise as the horse itself.

"Leo."

"Leif."

His judgmental tone is loud in my ears before he says another word.

Sure enough, he doesn't waste any time with the sarcasm. "You're here for the tournament? Thought you'd be halfway across the world by now. Chasing waves or something."

I clench my jaw. "I know Mother told you I'm here now. In Paris."

He scoffs, his voice sharp. "Oh, you're *here* now. And I'm supposed to care? What, because you showed up, everything's supposed to be fine?"

I feel the tension rising, my fingers itching around the mallet handle. "What's that supposed to mean?"

Leif fixes his piercing gaze on me, his eyes cold. "It means you're selfish, Leo. You left us—left the family—to travel, to surf, to do whatever it is you do, while the rest of us dealt with the reality of Father's situation. And now you waltz back in, expecting everything to fall into place."

I bite the inside of my cheek, the words bubbling up before I can stop them. "I needed time, Leif. To figure things out. And Father was better when I left."

"Figure things out?" He laughs, but there's no humor in it. "You're always figuring things out. The truth is, if it were me in line to be king, things would be different. I wouldn't run away."

Run away?

Is that what everyone thinks? That I'm running? I feel it like a punch in the gut.

Does Daisy think that too? Maybe she hasn't responded because she doesn't like how Grumpy McFadden rode away from his love after they put their lock on the bridge.

"You don't get it," I snap. "You think it's easy? You think I wanted this?"

"I don't care what you wanted," Leif says through gritted teeth. "I'm sick of your flaky personality, Leo. You don't get to leave when things get tough and expect us to clean up the mess."

His words cut deeper than I expected. Am I really that flaky? To Leif, to the family . . . to Daisy?

My blood boils, and before I can respond, Leif turns his gaze to James, who's been watching us closely, his face unreadable.

"You know I'm right," Leif says, his voice lowering as if trying to pull James to his side. "Tell him I'm right."

James crosses his arms, his gaze steady. He doesn't hesitate. "I'm not coming between you two. But my loyalty is to Leo—today, tomorrow, and always."

Leif clenches his jaw, looking between the two of us. His shoulders tense, and for a second, I see a flash of something in his eyes—something deeper, something I can't name—but then it's gone.

"You're a fool," Leif says, turning back to me. "You've had everything handed to you. And still, you throw it away."

I stare at him, the weight of his words hanging between us. "I'm here now," I say again, softer this time. But I wonder if I'm saying it more to myself. To convince myself that I'm not the one who runs away from things that matter.

Leif shakes his head, disgust clear on his face, and mounts his horse, riding off without another word.

I stand there, frozen, the sound of hooves echoing in the distance. James steps beside me, his hand resting on my shoulder.

"You okay, man?"

I exhale slowly, trying to clear the fog of frustration clouding my head. "Yeah. I'm fine."

But the truth is, I'm not sure I am—not when what Leif said is very close to what I've been thinking about myself, too.

"Don't let him get to you, Leo. You know it's what he does—and probably always will. He can't stand it."

"Stand what?"

"That the better brother will be king. Because we all know—Leif included—that if the timing were reversed, you wouldn't be bitter toward him."

"Of course not."

"That's what he hates."

I watch Leif slam the ball with his mallet as if he wishes it were my head.

I wish I could give him those fifteen minutes of life back.

I don't say it aloud because wishing for the impossible is a waste of a wish. There are many better things to put all my heart and soul into.

Starting with Plan D -- dusting off the royal card and throwing it down, with a simple question, "Daisy, do you want to be my princess?"

Maybe James is right. I need to cut to the chase (no polo pun intended).

Kingdom of Arandel

Chapter Thirty-Two

DAISY

I stand at the corner of our street, waiting for Jake. The morning is fresh, and I'm practically buzzing with excitement. Montmartre. I've read about it, daydreamed about it, and now, here I am, about to explore it. With Jake.

Suddenly, I hear the hum of a scooter engine, and I turn around to see Jake pulling up on the most adorable scooter I've ever seen.

A pink scooter.

I laugh out loud, shaking my head as he parks it right in front of me, a sheepish grin on his face. "You like it?"

"Are you kidding? It's perfect!"

"I tried to get one in green," he says, shrugging as he takes off his helmet. "But all they had was this beauty. So, I figured, what the hell."

I can't help but smile at the sight of it. "Jake, I *love* it."

He hands me a helmet. "Well, hop on, then. Let's see how much you love it when we're zoomin' up the hill."

I slide the helmet over my head, adjusting the strap, and climb onto the back of the scooter. My arms instinctively wrap around his waist, and I freeze for a moment, feeling the hardness of his abs under his jacket.

How does a philosophy major even have abs like these? Aren't they supposed to be all soft and bookish?

I shake my head, trying to focus on the day ahead instead of the warmth radiating from him. He glances back at me, his Southern drawl dripping with teasing. "Comfortable back there?"

I smile. "Yeah. I'm good."

With that, we're off, the scooter zipping through the narrow streets of Paris, weaving past pedestrians and parked cars. I feel the wind in my hair, and I can't help but laugh as we ride. It's like something straight out of a movie—Jake in front of me, the pink scooter, the world of Paris unfolding around us.

We zoom up the hill toward the Basilica de Sacré-Cœur, the gleaming white domes coming into view as we near the top. Jake parks the scooter at the base, and we both hop off, our legs a little wobbly from the ride.

"I can't believe this," I say, gazing up at the massive church in front of us. "It's even more beautiful in person."

Jake hands me my camera. "Well, we gotta capture it, don't we?"

We spend the next few minutes snapping pictures in front of the basilica before heading over to one of the little stalls nearby. Jake buys us crêpes, wrapped in triangles of wax paper, and we sit down on a bench to eat them. Mine is stuffed with Nutella, and I take a bite, savoring the rich, chocolatey goodness.

"Mm, this is so good," I mumble through a mouthful of crêpe.

Jake grins. "Told ya, Paris does it right."

After finishing our crêpes, we stroll through the winding streets of Montmartre, where the air is filled with the scent of fresh bread and the hum of artists sketching tourists on the sidewalks. It feels like every corner is a new discovery—like we've stepped into a postcard.

We wander through the squares where Van Gogh and the great painters used to hang out, drinking and discussing art. I try to imagine what it must've been like back then—sitting in a café, surrounded by talent and brilliance.

"Can you believe Van Gogh lived here?" I ask as we walk up to the house where he lived with his brother, Theo.

Jake shrugs, his arm brushing against mine. "Seems like the kinda place that would inspire someone. I mean, look at it. It's got magic in the air."

I snap a photo in front of the house, feeling like I'm capturing a piece of history. As we walk away, we stumble upon a group of people on a chocolate tour.

Jake nudges me, his voice low. "Wanna crash it?"

I laugh, shaking my head. "Are you serious?"

"Why not? We're already here."

Before I can protest, Jake pulls me along, and we blend in with the group as they move from shop to shop, tasting some of the best chocolate Paris has to offer. We manage to sneak a few samples, and by the end, we're both grinning like kids on Halloween, pockets stuffed with chocolate.

"That was amazing," I say, biting into a piece of dark chocolate.

Jake wipes his mouth, laughing. "You've got a little . . . right there."

I swipe at my cheek, embarrassed, but Jake just laughs again. "I was kiddin'. You're perfect."

I feel my face flush as we continue walking, our bags full of chocolate and our hearts full from the day. It's easy being around Jake. The way he teases, the way he smiles—it's all so natural, like we've been friends forever.

As we walk back to the scooter, the sun starts to dip below the rooftops of Paris, casting a golden glow over everything. I hop onto the back of the scooter, wrapping my arms around Jake's waist again.

This time, I don't think about his abs. I think about how lucky I am to be here, in this city, with someone who makes me laugh.

"Ready?" he asks, glancing back at me.

"Ready," I say, smiling.

And with that, we ride back down the hill, the city lights flickering to life around us.

Chapter Thirty-Three

DAISY

"So you don't like him in that way?" Lulu says when I tell her that Jake and I had a great time, but there was no love blooming in the air, no birds singing on our shoulders, and no golden light joining our souls as one.

"I get it," she says. "Friends."

"Exactly."

"Well, you still have Étienne."

I blush. "Yes. I think . . . ."

"What?"

"He's been . . . getting very cozy with me."

Lulu twirls her hands. "Define 'cozy' please. You Americans and your secret code words."

I laugh. Lulu and I are getting mani/pedis side by side and catching up on our news.

Lulu is excited that she got hired at her dream job with the doll dress designer. I still can't believe Lulu dresses dolls and gets paid for it.

"You literally play with dolls all day?"

She splashes water from her manicure bowl on me. "I don't play with the dolls. I prepare them for display."

"Oh no, my dear, you play with the dolls. I've been your roomie for only a few weeks, and I know you already."

She grins. "It's the best job in the world."

"Actually, I heard that an ice cream taster is the best job."

"Well, mine is a close second."

"I won't argue with that."

Lulu snorts with laughter, which cracks me up.

"Stop," I cry. "You're killing me."

Lulu wiggles her fingers at me, admiring the bright pink polish the nail tech is carefully applying.

"So, enough about me and my dolls—spill the details! What about you and the oh-so-gorgeous Étienne? You haven't told me about your *sketching date* in the Luxembourg Gardens yet."

I feel my cheeks heat up, and I try to play it cool, but I know I'm failing. "It was . . . spectacular."

Lulu raises an eyebrow, leaning in. "Spectacular? That's not the word I'd use for getting cozy, but I'm intrigued. Go on."

I smile, trying to decide where to start. "Well, we met at the entrance to the gardens, and it was like something out of a movie. The flowers, the fountains . . . Étienne was already there, sitting on a bench, sketchbook in hand."

Lulu tilts her head with a dreamy look. "Let me guess—dark curls falling into his eyes, looking all mysterious?"

I laugh. "Exactly. And of course, he looked like he belonged in a painting himself."

Lulu sighs dramatically. "How do you get to live in a romantic movie while I'm over here with my dolls?"

"Hey, you love those dolls!" I nudge her playfully.

"Don't change the subject. Tell me everything."

I bite my lip, a smile spreading across my face despite myself. "We walked through the gardens for a while, just talking. The flowers were blooming everywhere, and there were these little pathways that made it feel like we were the only two people in the world. It was perfect."

Lulu leans in, eyes sparkling. "And? What did you two talk about?"

"Everything and nothing. We talked about art, flowers, life in Paris. He was . . . close. Like, physically close. I could feel him beside me the whole time. There was this tension, you know? Like something was about to happen."

Lulu's eyes widen. "Oh, now you're talking. What happened next?"

I take a deep breath, remembering the moment as clearly as if I were still there. "We found this spot surrounded by flowers, just like we talked about. He asked if I was ready for my grand moment of being sketched."

"And were you?"

"I was trying to play it cool, but inside, I was a mess." I laugh softly. "He started sketching, and I couldn't take my eyes off him. The way he looked at me . . . like he was seeing something no one else ever had. It made me nervous, but also . . . excited."

Lulu fans herself. "Okay, keep going. Don't leave me hanging."

I blush harder, my heart racing just remembering it. "Then, while he was sketching, he stopped. He looked at me for a long moment, and I knew. I just *knew*."

"Knew what?"

"That he was going to kiss me."

Lulu gasps, her hands flying to her cheeks. "Daisy! Did he? Tell me he did."

I nod slowly, my stomach flipping just thinking about it. "He did. It was . . . my first kiss, Lulu. Ever."

Lulu's mouth drops open, and she reaches over to grab my arm. "Oh my God. Your *first kiss*?! In the Luxembourg Gardens with a gorgeous French artist? This is unreal."

I smile, but the memory hits me hard, and my heart twists. "It was . . . beautiful. He was gentle, but there was this intensity too, like he'd been waiting for that moment as long as I had."

Lulu stares at me, wide-eyed. "Okay, so . . . how did it feel? Was it everything you hoped?"

I hesitate, my emotions swirling. "It was. It really was."

"But?" Lulu asks, sensing the shift in my tone.

"But . . . it wasn't Leo."

Lulu's excitement dims, and she gives me a knowing look. "Ah. There it is."

I sigh, leaning back in my chair. "I know. I feel something for Étienne. I do. But no matter how perfect the moment was, or how beautiful the kiss, I couldn't help but think about Leo. I couldn't help but compare."

Lulu tilts her head. "Dais, that's normal. Leo was your first . . . love, in a way. Of course, you're going to think about him."

"Maybe," I say softly, staring at the ceiling. "But I just wish it didn't feel so complicated. I wish I could just . . . let go."

Lulu gives me a soft smile. "You will. In time. But for now, just enjoy it. You kissed Étienne, and that's huge. Don't overthink it."

I nod, trying to take her advice to heart, but deep down, I know. No one is Leo. And no kiss, no matter how perfect, is going to change that.

Chapter Thirty-Four

LEO

I jog through the streets of Paris, the cool morning air filling my lungs as I weave between early risers and narrow streets. James, true to his word, pedals behind me on a bicycle, keeping pace as we zigzag around sleepy pedestrians and street vendors setting up for the day.

"Not bad for a guy who hasn't been on a bike in years," James shouts, a grin spreading across his face.

I laugh, shaking my head. "Don't slow down now. We're just getting started."

I focus on my breathing, feeling the rhythm of the city waking up around me. I'm trying to clear my head, to stop thinking about her. About Daisy. It's why I dragged James out here. No more obsessing. No more stalking.

"What's for me will be for me," I say, more to myself than to James, repeating the mantra I've been telling myself for days now.

James pedals up beside me, giving me a side glance. "How very mature of you."

I smirk but don't respond. We continue running, the mist

rising off the pavement in soft, curling tendrils as the city shakes off the last traces of night. Paris in the morning has a magic to it—the quiet before the rush. I should be focusing on that. Not her.

And yet, just as I'm trying to push the thought of Daisy out of my mind, I see it.

A cute pink scooter pulls up at the stoplight ahead, coming to a halt.

No way.

My heart skips a beat as I notice the person driving it—Daisy, wearing the most adorable flowered helmet. She's right there. Less than ten feet away. I'm literally jogging in place, waiting for the light to change, and she's oblivious, her eyes focused ahead as if I don't even exist.

I freeze, barely able to believe it. She's so close I could reach out and tap her on the shoulder.

It's her. It's *really* her.

James rolls up beside me on his bike, noticing my sudden stop. "What's up? You lose a shoe or something?"

"She's right there," I whisper, barely able to keep my voice steady. My heart is pounding in my chest, but not from the run.

James squints at the pink scooter. "Who?"

"Daisy."

He blinks, then looks at me like I've lost my mind. "Leo, man . . . . You're seeing her everywhere these days."

I shake my head furiously. "No, I'm serious. *That's* her."

Before James can respond, the light changes. Daisy zooms off, the little scooter whirring through the street, disappearing around the corner.

Without thinking, I start sprinting after her, my feet pounding the pavement as I try to keep up. But she's too fast, too far. I stop, panting, watching as she vanishes into the city, leaving me standing there with nothing but the sound of my heartbeat in my ears.

I'm sure it was her. I *know* it was her.

James catches up to me, hopping off his bike and wiping his forehead. "You good, man? You look like you've seen a ghost."

I grab him by the shoulders, practically shaking him. "Did you see her? It was Daisy. I swear."

James raises an eyebrow, his voice calm. "Leo, I think you're losing it. You're seeing her everywhere. First at the party, now here."

"I'm not losing it," I insist, my pulse still racing. "It was *her*."

James lets out a long breath, rubbing the back of his neck. "Okay, even if it was . . . what's the plan, man? You gonna chase her all over Paris on foot?"

I shake my head, determination flaring inside me. "No. We're going to the Sorbonne."

James looks at me, bewildered. "The Sorbonne? How exactly are we supposed to pull that off?"

I grin, the adrenaline pumping through my veins. "I'm using my royal card."

James's face breaks into a smile, his eyes lighting up. "Oh, *now* we're talking. I'm in."

Chapter Thirty-Five

LEO

I drop my phone onto the couch and rub my temples. My mind is spinning, and no amount of exercise this morning cleared it up. Daisy was so close—right there at the stoplight. If I'd just turned a second faster or said something . . . .

James's lounging across from me, scrolling through his phone like he has no care in the world. I know he's waiting for me to say something. He always knows when I've got something on my mind.

I lean back, staring at the ceiling. "You ready for school?"

James raises an eyebrow without looking up. "You're serious?"

I nod. "Dead serious."

He puts down his phone, leaning forward. "You want me to go back to school now? You've been stalking your ex, jogging through Paris, and now you want to play student? Alright, alright. You've officially lost it."

I give him a look. "Come on, I'm not *that* bad."

James snorts. "Bro, I saw you sprint after a pink scooter this morning. You were practically drooling."

I groan, covering my face. "Okay, fine. But I saw her. I swear it was Daisy."

James leans back, arms crossed. "You keep saying that, but what's the plan, man? We just gonna hang out at the Sorbonne until she magically appears?"

I sit up straight, my pulse kicking up again. "That's exactly the plan. She's there, James. We know that for sure."

James raises an eyebrow. "And then what? When we finally see her face to face. She's living her life as a college student. You want her to drop all that and be your wife? In a cold, cold country?"

I ignore the sarcasm and stand up, pacing. "I need to see her, talk to her. She deserves an explanation."

James watches me for a beat, then sighs. "You keep talking about making amends. But isn't the endgame to tell her about all of this?" He gestures vaguely around the apartment, meaning my title, the family, the whole *royal package*.

I run a hand through my hair, frustrated. "I don't know yet. But first, I need to see her. The rest . . . we'll figure out."

James stands up, stretching. "Well, at least you have a plan now. Better than the whole 'stalk Daisy from a distance' thing you've been pulling."

I laugh, shaking my head. "Let's go before I change my mind."

He grins, grabbing his jacket. "Ah, the Sorbonne. Back to school we go. This ought to be fun. Do I get to pick my own courses?"

I ignore him as we head out of the apartment. I feel the tension in my chest ease, just a little. Maybe today will be the day. Maybe I'll finally get a chance to explain everything to Daisy.

Kingdom of Arandel

We're cruising through the streets of Paris in the back of the car, heading straight for the Sorbonne. I'm trying to stay cool, but the tension's starting to creep back in.

I'm going to be King of my country one day. I can't be losing my cool like this. I know people would say it's just a girl. But Daisy is not just a girl.

And I don't want to be King without her. I drop my face in my hands. "She's meant for me, James."

"I may make jokes about this search for Daisy, but I wish I felt about anyone like you do about her. I wish my heart could feel as strongly about anything. You've got a gift, man, and I'll help you to make this work out."

I stare at my best friend. "Thanks."

James leans over from the seat beside me and says in a low voice. "You know Leif goes to the Sorbonne, too, right? What if we run into him?"

I hadn't thought about that. I blink, realizing how lucky I've been so far. *Leif.* He's been in Paris all this time, and Daisy hasn't run into him yet. "I guess I'm lucky she hasn't. The last thing I need is for her to meet my twin brother before she sees me again."

James raises an eyebrow. "Lucky, huh?"

I shrug. "Look, it's fine. We're not there to cause trouble. We're just sitting in on a few classes to see if the Sorbonne is a fit for us."

James bursts out laughing. "Two princes walking into a college class? They didn't think that was weird?"

I grin. "They said yes, didn't they? That's all that matters. We get to sit in on classes."

He shakes his head, still laughing. "This is gonna be fun."

Just then, James taps the driver's shoulder. "Stop here. I need to pick something up."

I give him a look. "What? You planning a shopping spree?"

He hops out of the car before I can protest, disappearing into a small store. I sit back, staring out the window, my thoughts slipping back to Daisy. I can still picture her on that scooter, so close and yet so far.

Minutes later, James returns, and he's carrying a massive, bulging bag. I raise an eyebrow. "What's all this?"

He starts unloading the stuff into the backseat, and I can't help but chuckle. Backpacks, books, pens, and even two Sorbonne sweatshirts tumble out of the bag.

"Now we're ready," he says with a satisfied grin.

I hold up one of the sweatshirts, the Sorbonne logo proudly displayed on the front. "We're wearing matching shirts now?"

He grins back at me. "We gotta fit in, dude. Can't be princes today. We're just regular students."

I roll my eyes but can't help the smile tugging at my lips. James always has a way of turning serious moments into something lighter. But then I pull out my phone and show him a picture of Daisy.

"This is her," I say, my voice more serious now. "Find her and call me. That's the mission."

James studies the photo for a moment, then nods. "Got it. Operation Find Daisy is officially underway."

Kingdom of Arandel

Chapter Thirty-Six

DAISY

I pull up to the school and park my scooter in the designated spot, but my mind is far from here. The entire ride, I kept thinking the same thing, over and over.

I saw him. I saw Leo.

It couldn't have been him . . . could it? The guy jogging next to my scooter at the stoplight—he had Leo's build, his walk. That casual but athletic stride. It had to be him. But I'm in Paris. He's . . . somewhere else, right?

I must be going crazy. I didn't dare turn and stare. I couldn't just check him out through my helmet's visor like some creep.

What if it wasn't him, and the guy thought I wanted to run him over? No, I kept my eyes straight ahead and focused on the road, but my heart wouldn't stop pounding.

I take off my helmet and run my fingers through my hair, trying to shake the feeling.

Just then, Étienne appears from the building, his face lighting up when he spots me. "Daisy! Is this your new ride?"

I force a smile, still trying to focus. "Yeah, I bought it after riding one this weekend. It's used, but I got a pretty good deal on an online marketplace."

He walks over, admiring the scooter with a smile. "It suits you. Very . . . free-spirited."

I laugh softly. "That's what I'm going for. Plus, it makes getting around Paris a lot easier."

We start walking toward the entrance, and Étienne falls into step beside me. "So, have you considered what your project will be for our Art History final? It's two-thirds of our grade."

I shake my head. "I honestly can't grasp what he's asking us to do. Blend the old with the new?"

Étienne smiles. "Choose a project that blends Paris itself, with its layers of history overlaid by modernity, and embody the duel between the old (permanent) and the new (ephemeral)."

"Exactly, what does that mean!" I cry, forgetting my distress over the possible Leo sighting.

Étienne's gorgeous dark hair falls in his eyes. I so want to sweep it away.

For real, Daisy, you want to touch Étienne when you were just swooning over Leo?"

I frown at myself.

"What's wrong?"

How can I explain to Étienne, who has been nothing but sweet to me, that I'm seeing Leo's ghost all over Paris? I'd sound crazy.

"Nothing," I wave my hand in the air. "Let's go inside."

I lock my scooter and pat its pretty pink seat. "You are gorgeous," I whisper to my new best friend.

"Are you talking to your scooter?" Étienne's head tilts in a puzzled way. I've learned it's not always because he's puzzled. Sometimes, he's thinking about how to sketch a scene.

As we walk down the hallowed halls of Sorbonne's centuries-old building, I admire the walls and the ceiling. "We are already in a layer of history right here," I murmur.

"Absolutely," Étienne says, not looking as interested in our surroundings as much as in me.

"So, what are you going to do? I'm sure you already have a lot of ideas. You're an artist."

Étienne begins talking about how art can embody the old with the new. Or how we can use old art to inspire new ones.

"He may be suggesting we look into how digital art is replacing the traditional, older art forms."

I nod, trying to keep up with the conversation, but my mind is racing with the image of the jogger. His blond hair, the way he carried himself—it couldn't be a coincidence.

I glance at Étienne as he talks, something about capturing beauty, which is the essence of any art.

I almost walk into a pillar. He's so handsome. How did I get lucky for the one guy everyone likes to be talking to me?

He guides me away from a face plant and keeps a hand on the small of my back.

"What? I'm sorry," I ask, realizing he said my name.

"You! I want to paint you. I think you embody the old with the new."

"Me? How?"

But I'm not listening to him because I'm feeling that I missed something important. Something more than just seeing someone who looked like Leo. It's like a weight in my chest, a nagging thought that won't go away.

Chapter Thirty-Seven

DAISY

"You okay?" Étienne asks, bending down to look into my eyes.

I blink, snapping back to the moment. "Yeah, sorry. I'm just a little distracted."

He turns me around to face him. Students flow by us like a rushing river. Classes have started, including ours.

But Étienne does not seem to be in a rush at all. The concern in his eyes pierces me. I was so rude by not listening to him.

"Talk to me, Daisy. I care about you." He swipes a tendril of my hair back and puts his hands on my shoulders. "I'm here for you."

I gulp. What woman wouldn't want to hear these words? What's wrong with me? Why can't I feel about Étienne the way I felt about Leo?

Why can't I get with the program? Be a normal girl who likes a guy who likes her back, who wants to paint me, for heaven's sake.

I'm sick in the head.

Emerald was right. I can't have the fairy tale.

The fairy tale would be Leo appearing out of nowhere, and we'd fall in love in Paris. I'd stroll along the Seine arm in arm with him, we'd kiss on the Pont des Arts, lock a love lock there together, and promise we'd never be apart. Ever.

That is the freaking fairy tale. That's the story I've been clinging to in my head and heart.

But girlfriend, that story is *not* happening. Everyone knows it but me.

I stare into Étienne's dark eyes and reach up to stroke his hair. "You are wonderful, Étienne. Thank you for being here for me."

He nods, his gaze soft. "I would like to be more."

I swallow hard. "Okay," I say, a little more firmly than I feel. "Let's be more."

A smile breaks across his face, wider and brighter than I've ever seen before.

"Really? I thought you might have a boyfriend back home. You always looked sad, like you were missing someone."

"Not always," I protest gently.

"No, not always," he agrees, "but whenever I got close to you, there was a shimmer in your eyes that said, *don't get too close—I'm taken*."

I step back, surprised, and grasp his hands. "Really? My eyes said that?"

He nods, his thumb brushing the top of my knuckles. "*Oui.* It's like you were here with me, but part of you was somewhere else. Or maybe . . . with someone else."

I swallow, a lump forming in my throat as I realize how perceptive he is. He sees more than I've been willing to admit. "I . . . I didn't know I was giving that off."

Étienne's dark eyes search mine, and I feel a softness there, a gentleness that reminds me of the safety I crave. But safety isn't always what sets the heart on fire, is it?

"It's okay," he says quietly. "I didn't push, because I didn't want to intrude. But I'm here, Daisy. If you want to let someone in."

I blink back the sudden prickle of tears. It feels like he's asking for more than just a date, more than just casual moments together. He's asking for a space in my heart I've kept closed off, waiting for someone else. Someone who may never come back.

"I want to," I whisper, almost to myself, testing the words, unsure if they're true. But when I see the hope flicker in his eyes, something shifts.

"I want to try, Étienne."

His smile returns, softer this time, like he's trying to contain his excitement. He steps closer, our hands still connected. "We don't have to rush. Let's just see where this takes us. One step at a time."

I nod, but there's a heaviness in my chest that won't go away. I know what he means, and I appreciate his patience, but can I really give him a chance?

Can I let go of Leo enough to let someone else in?

Étienne leans down, and for a moment, I'm breathless. Is he going to kiss me?

Instead, he brushes his lips softly against my forehead, a gesture so sweet and tender it nearly brings me to tears. He's not pushing, not forcing anything. He's giving me the space I didn't know I needed.

When he pulls back, there's a hint of vulnerability in his eyes, as if he's as unsure as I am about what's happening between us.

Chapter Thirty-Eight

DAISY

Like a rainbow appearing unexpectedly, Étienne changes the mood.

"Let's play hockey." His eyes light up.

"*Hockey?*"

He nods enthusiastically. "Isn't that what Americans say? When they want to skip a class or work?"

"Ah!" I laugh with relief. "It's *hookey.*"

"Oh, not hockey?"

"No, and what do you have in mind?" I wink, suggestively like I've seen Corrine do to Salvador.

Étienne blinks as if he can't believe it. Me, Daisy Walker, is winking at him.

"Um . . . let's skip our class and grab a coffee," he says, his voice light and playful. "Then see where it goes."

"*Oh la la,*" I whisper. "Yes, let's."

Okay, who is this Jezebel who has kidnapped Daisy? I all but skip outside the doors of Sorbonne, holding his hand.

When I stop next to my scooter, he shakes his head. "It's a beautiful day, and we should enjoy it. Let's walk."

We walk together, holding hands, through the bustling streets of Paris.

The leaves are starting to turn, their edges golden and red, fluttering down onto the cobblestone paths.

We stop at the Shakespeare and Company bookstore and browse amongst the stacks of books for over an hour, him in the arts section and me in romance.

When our stomachs growl, we order sandwiches and sodas at the attached cafe and sit outside in the sunshine as a line forms to get into the famous bookshop.

"I've never seen a line to get into a bookstore except in Paris," Étienne says proudly.

"I have."

"Really, where?"

Can I talk about Porto without crying? This is my test, I figure. I swallow the lump in my throat.

"In Porto, Portugal. When visiting my sister last year (do not mention Leo!), there was always a long line to get into the Harry Potter bookstore. Its real name is *Livraria Lello,* and it's considered the world's most beautiful bookstore. It's stunning."

"Why is it called the Harry Potter bookstore?"

"Because J.K. Rowling lived in Porto. And supposedly, she conceived of the Harry Potter universe there because she drank coffee in that bookstore. Everyday!"

"Amazing, isn't it?"

"What is?" I ask, trying not to let my memory flow from the *Livraria Lello* to the other sights Leo and I visited together in Porto.

"How influential and inspiring a bookstore can be to our lives. This one here," he points at the Shakespeare & Co. store, "welcomed thousands of young writers and intellectuals to stay overnight for free and create."

"I didn't know that," I give the shop another appreciative look.

"And look at how popular it still is. Isn't that an example of how old art and new art coexist?"

"Yes," I exclaim. A kernel of an idea plants itself in my mind of how to use my love locks for my art history project.

But first, I turn my attention to Étienne as he describes why he wants me to be the subject of his class project.

I'm flattered but confused. "How would it work?"

He leans forward, arms leaning on the little table. I am mesmerized by his intensity.

"I would love to paint you in front of an old Parisian landmark with a lot of history, like the Notre Dame Cathedral, which is right across the bridge from where we're sitting. Or the Eiffel Tower."

I listen as he sketches in the air what he's picturing.

"I'd paint the background in muted, classic colors, reflecting the timelessness of old Paris. But for you, Daisy, I could use bright, vibrant, and almost impressionistic colors to suggest movement, life, and the fleeting nature of a moment in time."

"Wow! That sounds unreal."

"*Au contraire,* it would be very real."

I tell him my idea about using the love locks.

"I'm thinking of creating a virtual bridge using digital art, where the old and new can come together.

"I'll take photos of the old locks being removed from the real bridge, and digitally recreate them on this virtual bridge. People could 'buy' new locks to add as well, with their initials or messages, just like they did on the Pont des Arts.

"When you click on a lock, you'd be able to read the story behind it—the couple's love story, why they placed the lock, and even an update on where they are now, if they want to share.

"It's a way to preserve both the old, physical love stories and create new ones. I've already started gathering interest through my Instagram page, and people want to share their stories. It's like I'm creating a digital community of love lock keepers."

"*Incroyable!*"

I blush. "It's just an idea. I'm not good at digital art, but I can do it with my graphic design software."

"I can't believe you've already started your art project. It makes the rest of us look like we are slackers."

"I thought you knew," I say.

"No. I didn't. But it's so . . . community-minded. Much better than any of the ideas I've heard, including mine."

"Really?"

He nods.

A whizz of excitement sparks through me. "Thanks."

"So, are the locks representing both old and new?"

"Yes," I say excitedly. "The lock itself represents . . . I don't know . . . a *promise* of permanence. Something old that lasts forever. But as we all know . . . (me especially), love can be fleeting. And with the locks being cut off the bridge, they symbolize how something permanent or older can be replaced by something newer."

The more I talk, the more the truth hits me.

My love for Leo can be . . . *is* . . . like an older fleeting love story. I can lock it away on the virtual bridge and be done with it. Replace it with something newer . . . .

"Yeah, right," I mumble. "Easy peasy."

"How will people pay for a lock?"

"Hmmm . . . I didn't get that far."

I sip my soda quietly.

"Donations," I say unexpectedly. "People can donate to a cause and put their lock and love story on the virtual bridge!"

"Nice," Étienne nods. "It's getting better and better. What cause?"

I don't hesitate. "Education, teachers, centers that teach everything from literacy to sports, in Senegal's rural towns."

"Okay, that's specific."

"And necessary. My roommate Lulu has told me about the Senegal NGOs she donates to weekly. I will, too."

Étienne sits back. "Now I know why I wanted to paint you as soon as I saw you. You are a golden flower, Daisy. Inside and out."

"Please, I'm just human with a lot of flaws. My sister Emerald is the planet's activist."

"You are changing lives too, Here in Paris. Soon, in Senegal. And around the world. With your love for love."

Tears form in my eyes. Is he right?

Am I growing up and doing something meaningful with my love for romance and fairy tales?

I clutch my hands together. "Thank you, Étienne. For listening and helping me see a path ahead."

"You were already on the path. I'm just lucky to be on your way."

We leave the bookstore's cafe and continue our stroll around the neighborhood. I feel light and carefree. Étienne sees me more clearly than I see myself.

I glance over at him as he talks about a new art exhibition opening next week, his eyes bright with excitement. "We must go."

He's everything I should want. He's here. He's real. He's willing to be mine.

And as we walk past the couples holding hands, past the bridges with love locks glittering in the sun, I can't help but wonder:

Is this me making my own fairy tale?

Chapter Thirty-Nine

LEO

We pull up in front of the Sorbonne, and my heart is pounding in my chest. I grip the handle of the car door, frozen for a second. This is it.

I'm going to talk to my sweet Daisy again.

I can feel it.

James, sitting beside me, glances over, his eyebrows furrowed as if he's worried about me.

But James is not a worrier by nature, which means it's serious. I've become a cause of concern for my best friend.

"Before we go out there," I say, as if we're heading to battle, "I want to thank you for . . . you know . . . being here with me. You could be surfing instead. I appreciate it."

His face splinters into a smile. "I better be the best man at your wedding."

I nod, my throat tight. "I promise. I just hope I'm not too late."

"Too late for what? We're here now. Just go talk to her."

Easier said than done. I've been imagining this moment for months, replaying it repeatedly. What will I say? How will she react? Does she even want to see me after all this time?

I push the door open and step out onto the sidewalk.

Students are milling about, chatting in groups, some rushing to class. I scan the crowd, searching for that familiar flash of curly hair, that smile I've missed so much.

All I see are strangers, hurrying past without a second glance.

James steps up beside me, pulling a sweatshirt from his bag. "Here, put this on. We gotta blend in."

I pull the Sorbonne sweatshirt over my head, grateful for the distraction. "You really think this will work?"

He grins. "Worth a shot. Now come on, let's find her."

We start walking toward the main entrance, but just as I'm about to step inside, I freeze. There she is.

Daisy.

She's standing at the top of the outside stairs, laughing, her dark curls bouncing in the sunlight. My heart stumbles in my chest at the sight of her. She looks even more beautiful than I remember. But then I see him.

I step backward into the shadow of the building.

"What now?" James mutters. "Not him again. Please let me take him . . . I mean, distract him away from Daisy."

"Shhh," I whisper as they walk down the stairs. "Dude is standing right next to her. Are they holding hands?" Sweat drips off me like bullets.

"Yes, man, they are. Now, please let me go handle this."

I push Thanbdo back. "We're in the middle of Paris. We're not starting any fights."

James sucks his teeth. "I hate Paris."

"I almost agree."

The world tilts for a second as I watch them. My stomach clenches, and I can't tear my eyes away. They start walking, hand in hand, down the street, talking, laughing like there's no one else around.

It hits me like a punch to the gut. She's moved on. Maybe she doesn't even think about me anymore.

"Damn," James murmurs beside me. "That's rough."

I swallow, my throat dry. "Yeah. Tell me about it."

James shifts, clearly uncomfortable with the weight of the moment. "You wanna—"

"No," I cut him off, my voice tight. "I just . . . I need to see where they're going."

We hang back, following them at a distance. I can't believe I'm stalking her again. It's like I have no willpower. And no dignity. I'm a freaking King!

But no amount of logic or reasoning can stop me.

Not when my heart hurts like this.

It aches with every step they take, their fingers laced together like it's the most natural thing in the world.

The worst part is how she's looking at him . . . I remember when she used to look at me like that.

The guy says something, and she laughs, the sound like a knife twisting in my chest.

I don't even know this guy, but right now, I hate him. Not because he's done anything wrong—but because he's with her. And I'm not.

"Leo," James says softly, breaking the silence. "You good?"

"I don't know, man," I admit, my voice low. "I thought I'd be ready for this. But seeing her like that, with him . . . . It hurts more than I thought it would."

James's quiet for a moment before he sighs. "Look, maybe she's happy right now. But that doesn't mean it's over for you two. You haven't even talked to her yet. You don't know what's going on."

I nod, but my chest feels tight. "What if she doesn't want to talk to me? I wouldn't blame her. What the hell *was* I thinking?"

"Yeah, what were you thinking?"

"That I didn't want to hold her back. Or myself. We had separate lives and paths. Truth is . . . I didn't realize how much she meant to me. I was a fool. Plain and simple. How could I imagine Daisy would hold me back? She's the blood in my veins."

James grabs my shoulders. "There's only one way to find out if she feels the same way for you. You said how you guys stayed in touch for a while, talked every day, had inside jokes, and were becoming besties."

"Yeah."

"Well, that connection doesn't just disappear."

I raise my eyes, blinded by tears at him. I'm not afraid for James to see my vulnerability.

He's seen me cry when I was homesick, and when Leif was a monster to me. He's seen me bawl when I fell and broke my arm at football. James knows me better than I know myself.

Daisy and Étienne have disappeared around a corner. I take a deep breath, trying to steady myself. "I can't lose her, James. I can't."

"Then don't," he says simply. "But you gotta figure out what you want, Leo. You want to fight for her? Or walk away?"

I clench my fists, watching the empty street. "I want to fight for her."

James pats my shoulder. "Good. Now, let's figure out how we're gonna do this. Once and for all. You are truly like that Prince of Denmark. The one who couldn't make up his mind. Who waffled back and forth."

"Hamlet?"

"Yes, him. What's up with you, Scandinavian royalty? I swear."

"You know me, James. I've never been like this before."

"I know. But then you never loved any girl before either."

"It's scary. Love makes you lose yourself a little," I confess.

"Remind me to never fall in love."

As we turn back toward the car, I make up my mind. I'm going to show Daisy I love her. Show her I am the man for her.

And I'm not leaving until she knows the truth—about me, about us, about everything.

Chapter Forty

LEO

I stretch out on the couch, my mind spinning as I stare up at the ceiling. James lounges next to me, scrolling through his phone like he's got all the time in the world. It's frustrating. I'm in crisis mode, and my best friend looks like he's waiting for his nails to dry.

"Okay, man," James finally says, snapping his fingers. "Let's do this. How are we gonna win Daisy back?"

I sigh, rubbing my temples. "That's the question, isn't it? I need something big, something she'll remember."

James sits up, grinning. "What does Daisy like? What does she love? You've got to figure out what really matters to her."

I think back, trying to remember everything about her. Then it hits me. "Wait . . . when Daisy was helping her sister Corrine with her love story, she made her sit through an entire romantic comedy movie marathon."

James's eyebrows shoot up, and he bursts out laughing. "You're saying we should watch romcoms? Bro, you're killing me."

I groan, shaking my head. "I'm serious, man. She believes in all that stuff. Maybe there's something in those movies that can help."

James wipes a fake tear from his eye, still grinning. "This is too good. Prince Leo watching romcoms to win his girl back. I never thought I'd see the day."

I punch him lightly in the arm. "Just help me pick some movies."

We scroll through options until we finally settle on a few classic romcoms, starting with *You've Got Mail*.

As we watch, I can feel James getting more into it than he's willing to admit, laughing at the cheesy moments and groaning at the misunderstandings.

By the time we hit *Sleepless in Seattle*, we're both pretty invested; our feet are up on the coffee table, our arms are crossed, and our heads are tilted like we're urging Tom Hanks to do the right thing.

"The tension is worse than in an action movie," James says incredulously. "Who knew?"

When the credits roll at the end, James and I let out loud sighs of relief.

"Happy ever after prevails," I say. "Hopefully for me, too."

"So, Tom Hanks and Meg Ryan," James says, waving at the screen, "they're supposed to meet at the top of the Empire State Building?"

I nod, staring at the TV, but my mind's racing. "Yeah, it's the big moment. The grand gesture. He goes all the way up there, hoping she'll still be there."

James leans back, throwing his arm over the back of the couch. "And you think Daisy's waiting for her own grand gesture?"

I turn to him, something clicking in my brain. "That's exactly it. She's talked about this stuff before. The grand gesture—it's like this moment where everything comes together. You should have seen how Daisy got her sister to dress up for that moment. We were on a football field in Portugal. Plenty of thought went into it. Trust me, I even helped Corrine with her outfit."

James smirks. "Okay, I ain't asking how you helped. Let's focus on now. What are you thinking? You gonna pull a Tom Hanks and get Daisy to meet you somewhere?"

I sit up straight, my heart pounding with excitement. "The Eiffel Tower. It's gotta be the Eiffel Tower. That's the Paris version of the Empire State Building."

James raises an eyebrow. "You could always just buy the Pont des Arts bridge, man. Your country's loaded, you can save all those precious locks for Daisy."

I laugh, shaking my head. "I'm not buying a bridge, James. Daisy doesn't want me to throw money at her problems. That's not who she is."

James shrugs. "I mean, it'd be a pretty grand gesture. But I get it. No bridge. So, what's the plan?"

I stand up, pacing the room. "I've got to figure out how to get her there. To the Eiffel Tower. It's the only place that's big enough, important enough."

James crosses his arms, looking thoughtful for once. "You could send her another message. Something cryptic. Make her curious."

I snap my fingers, a grin spreading across my face. "Yes! I'll leave her a message. Something like . . . meet the love of your life at the top of the Eiffel Tower at 10 p.m."

James groans. "If we have to go that route, it might as well be as cheesy as possible. That's straight out of a romcom movie. She'll have to know it's from somebody who knows her well."

I nod, the excitement building. This is it. This is the plan. It's crazy, sure, but Daisy believes in fairy tales, and this is the grand gesture she'd want. I just hope she'll show up."

James nods hesitantly. "We already tried a Plan A, B, C and I think D? So, this is Plan E?"

"I didn't use Plan D—the royal card. But yes, if you're keeping track, this is Plan E." I cringe.

We stare at each other.

James clears his throat. "I hate to point out. But for two highly trained strategists as ourselves, we sure are letting one girl take us down."

"Who's we?" I ask, arching an eyebrow. "You're coming with me to my big 'I love you' moment?"

He sucks his teeth. "Duh! I'll be videotaping the reunion. For your future kids who won't believe Mommy and Daddy could be so dense."

I laugh, feeling more alive than I have in weeks. "No more plans. She'll come. I know she will."

"Here's to hoping." James grabs the remote and clicks off the TV.

"Well, if this doesn't work, you could always imitate *Notting Hill* next and show up in some bookstore, all '*I'm just a prince, standing in front of a girl*.'"

I roll my eyes, but deep down, I'm buzzing with excitement. Plan E's in motion. Now, all I need is for Daisy to believe in it.

Chapter Forty-One

DAISY

Most days should end at their peak point so you can slide under the covers, cuddle up with a warm and fuzzy blanket, and let your mind wander over the moments you want to hold dear forever.

Later, after what happened next, I wished I had jumped on my scooter and gone back to my and Lulu's apartment and done just that.

I could have poured a glass of delicious champagne and relaxed on our balcony. Lulu and I could have discussed my outing with Étienne.

I could have shared how I felt as if I was on my way to creating my own fairy tale instead of waiting for Leo to ride up on a white horse and be my hero.

Lulu would have looked proud, as if her subtle teachings were finally sinking in.

But then fate had to go and drop a bomb on my head.

And now, hours later, sitting on my bed crying my eyes out, I wonder if there was a way for me to know. Had I been blind? Had

I missed some serious red flags?

Was I so naive or trusting that I let my belief in true love and finding "The One" derail me?

It happens in all the best films. The girl always finds The One. He doesn't have to be perfect; he just has to be The One for her.

But how can someone so right for me be so wrong? That is what I am sitting here thinking while tears soak my pajama top.

I'm too sad to call my sisters. Emerald's smug voice would say, "I told you so."

Ava's gentle voice would be filled with compassion. Bridget and Corrine's voices would swing between pity for me and anger at whoever made me feel like this. Leo.

And Lulu! I have to avoid her too, because she would do something drastic.

So, it's just me alone with my thoughts racing around and around as I ask myself how I could be so clueless.

THIS IS WHAT HAPPENED.

After spending an enlightening and sort of romantic day together, Étienne and I returned to the Sorbonne. He wanted to pick up his art supplies, and I wanted to go to my European History class. It's the last class of the day, but it's my favorite one.

The professor tells a lot of anecdotes with unique facts about history, like that Florence was the first city in Europe to have fully paved streets. I loved sharing that with Ava who lived in Florence for six months.

Or that the Notre Dame Cathedral, over 860 years old, which I pass every day, is the most visited attraction in Europe.

We spent a whole week discussing the Silk Road trade routes and how travelers and merchants exchanged ideas, philosophies, art forms, and architectural styles between East and West, influencing European art, literature, and science.

The importance of travel!

Maxine is also in the class, and we sit and chat about school, boys, and our favorite parts of Paris, before class starts.

Today, I rushed in too late for our usual chat.

She tapped an imaginary watch on her wrist as I slid into a seat next to her.

"Where have you been? You weren't in Art History?" Maxine is from a small town hours from Paris. She told me once that she always feels as if she's missing out. She has that whole FOMO malady.

I smiled at her and reassured her she didn't miss anything. "Well, you sort of missed that Étienne and I went out."

She squealed, and I had to hush her as the professor started talking.

I yanked off my sweater because the room was hot. Or maybe I was heated by the fast-paced walk Étienne and I took to get back to school.

"Étienne wasn't in class either. I should have known." She crinkled her nose in a sweet, curious way. "Are you two . . . ."

"Shhh," I whispered. "We're trekking the Roman Road now." I pointed to the images on the board.

Maxine pushed her notebook toward me. She'd written, "Étienne and you?" Surrounded by hearts.

I stifled a giggle. I tilted my head from side to side. "Maybe," I wrote back.

Maxine nodded as if she appreciated the information. "I want to be you when I grow up. Did you kiss?"

Redness suffused my cheeks. I nodded.

"Is he as intense as he seems?"

"More," I whispered. "But also . . . authentic."

She sighed. "The best kind of man."

"Yup," I whispered, remembering my failures with Jackson Banza in high school . . . and now Leo Aldebrand.

The rest of the class was a deep dive into how the phrase "*All roads lead to Rome*" was coined.

All the feeder roads in other European countries and provinces lead to the Roman headquarters.

Interestingly, the professor talked about how the Roman road is still used in Southern France and was inspired by the myth of Hercules wanting to connect Spain to Sicily.

"We should go see it," Maxine said. "It's only a train ride away."

"Yes, we should," I agreed. Discovering other parts of France was on the list that Emerald had made me make before leaving Maine.

When class was over, Maxine and I chatted about that trip. Everything seemed so right.

A possible boyfriend in Étienne. A friend in Maxine. A field trip of sorts to see France by train. My day could have stopped right there.

Chapter Forty-Two

DAISY

But it seems that life is capable of offering you joy and heartbreak all at once.

What happened next may have been inevitable. But I sure as heck didn't see it coming.

Fate had set up the chessboard of our lives to lead to this moment where the queen (me) would be captured. Or instead, the pawn (also me) would be nuked. In either case, I was disposed of.

As we walked down the hallway of the Sorbonne, Maxine congratulated me on conquering the mysterious Étienne.

"It's not like that," I said, the familiar reddish color burning my face. "We're just starting to get to know each other."

"Is he going to paint you?" she asked. "Will you be his muse?"

I couldn't help but think she was more romantic than I was. And that's saying a lot.

"I'm not his muse," I laughed. "But he might paint me. We'll see."

Maxine started talking about Camille Claudel, the famous

muse of the French sculptor Rodin. I was laughing at her ridiculous comparisons to Étienne and me when I saw the face haunting me all over Paris.

I stopped dead in my tracks. Maxine stopped alongside me.

"What's wrong?"

"Leo?" I heard the name strangled on my breath.

Maxine gripped my arm. "Daisy. You look like you're going to faint."

I stumbled and held onto her arm. "Do you see him?"

Maxine looked around, "Who?"

"Him," I whispered. "That blond guy. Standing over there."

Maxine stared at where I was pointing. "Yes, I see him. He goes to school here. I think he was at your party."

"You saw him there too, right? I wasn't imagining it."

"Daisy, you want to sit down?"

"No," I shook my head. "I'm going to talk to him." I shrugged off her hand and strode with purpose toward Leo. He seemed oblivious to my presence.

While I've been longing to see him again, he's always been here like nothing ever happened between us.

I mean, nothing physical happened. But a lot of emotional stuff did. I did not imagine that.

I stopped when I got close enough to talk without shouting. Before I could say a word, Leo turned toward me.

He was standing with his hands in his pockets, a tailored jacket hugging his frame, casually fashionable. That was not how Leo looked or stood.

"Hi, it's you. Your name is Daisy, right? I was hoping you would call me. I didn't know how to reach you. But I left my number with your roommate."

"What?"

I shook my head. His voice sounded too deep. Maybe he had a cold or was getting over one.

And he didn't remember my name! Red hot smoke blew out my ears.

"How dare you?"

Leo's eyes opened wide. He swiped a hand through his blond hair, and tufts stuck up. As if highly gelled. Unlike the Leo I'd known, whose hair was usually plastered with salt water or blowing freely about.

"You've changed," I said softly. "You don't know me."

Leo stepped toward me. "But I'd like to." He stuck out a hand as if to introduce himself.

As if we hadn't spent many hours together side by side, laughing and talking, going to a football match, or a New Year's Eve party together.

Tears flooded my soul. But I refused to cry in front of him.

"We're strangers now? After months of talking on the phone. You're going to act like you don't know me?" Pain was rampant in my tone.

I couldn't help that. I was hurt. I was very, very hurt.

The blue eyes I knew so well, the ones I dreamt about, shifted in color. They turned a stormy grey.

A voice I never heard Leo use spoke coldly, "I see. He has you too. He has everything. Damn it, Leo."

"What?"

He all but snarled, "I am not your precious Leopold Montclair. I am Leif, his twin brother. The *younger* twin."

I stumbled back. His words all but slapped me in my face.

I would have fallen if Maxine hadn't looped one of my arms under hers and held me close to her side. Even though I am twice her size, she held onto me.

"Twins?" I exclaimed. "You are Leo's twin?"

I wasn't sure what hurt more. That Leo had kept such a big secret from me.

Or that all my Leo sightings in Paris were his brother Leif instead.

I didn't know until that moment, but I'd been holding onto the notion that Leo was here. Now, that possibility was out the window, and I felt he had deserted me all over again.

"This is too much, I cried. "How could he do this? Where is he?"

To say I wanted to take out my pain on Leif is an understatement. He was here. He looked like Leo. He was Leo, as far as I was concerned.

But Leif shook his head. "Once again, my loser brother has done his magic. Wrecking havoc where he goes. I don't know your story with him, Daisy, but if I were you, I'd forget him."

A sob escaped my lips.

"I'm sorry," Leif said and turned to walk away.

"Why would he do this?" I asked shamelessly, longing for an answer.

"Because he can. He has supreme authority," Leif said, walking off in the same body, with the same face, but not the man I had longed for.

"What does that mean?" I wailed pitifully.

Maxine's face was pale as she put her arms around my shaking shoulders. "Don't cry, Daisy. Whoever this Leo is, he's not worth it. And you have Étienne. I bet Étienne is one hundred times better than Leo."

We walked to the bathroom, where I tried to dry my tears and stop hiccuping. I had a flashback to being in a bathroom with my older sister Bridget at a dance in high school, where I was crying over another guy.

How could I be here again? Different bathroom, and a different boy, but the same feelings of hurt and rejection.

I was beginning to see why Bridget used to swear off love. It was too painful.

Afterward, Maxine made me sit at a nearby café and drink strong coffee. She held my hand and comforted me with talk about our trip to Southern France.

My head reeled with the knowledge that I didn't know Leo at all. I thought he was Leo Aldebrand. But his twin says it's Leo . . . or Leopold . . . Montclair.

Leo never mentioned me to his brother, so I was never anyone special to him at all. Meanwhile, I'd told everyone—my sisters, my father, my cousins—about Leo.

"I feel sick," I mumbled to Maxine.

My stomach, my head. *Everything* hurt.

I could barely swallow the coffee. Adrenaline was still racing through me. I was overcome with the freeze-or-flee response.

And I wanted to flee.

I wanted to scream out loud.

I wanted to pound my fists on the floor and die.

Can you die of a betrayal?

After we paid for the coffee and returned to the school, I faked being okay so Maxine would let me ride my scooter home.

Whatever dignity I had was long gone.

She hugged me tight.

I climbed aboard my pink scooter and rode home. Tears threatened to blind me.

Not even my cute pink scooter helped me feel better. The sadness and devastation of Leo's betrayal, his lies by omissions, and his disconnect from me were too overwhelming.

It was in that moment—that realization that all was lost with Leo—that I understood something else.

I was lost without him.

He was my dream.

I'd been holding on to the idea that we'd find each other again. He'd contact me, tell me something terrible happened, but now it's better, and we'd dance and sing and eat and drink and fall in love, whether in Paris or somewhere else in the world.

I thought we belonged together. I truly believed that.

But now, my heart feels as if it's been ripped right out of my chest.

Leo is not coming back. There is no true love. There is no happily ever after. There is no fairy tale.

And there will never be a love lock for Daisy and Leo.

Chapter Forty-Three

LEO

The phone rings, slicing through the stillness of the apartment, and I don't even glance at the screen before answering, my mind going over every detail of my and Daisy's epic second chance meet cute.

James and I've got all the romcom lingo down.

The plan's finalized, the reunion set—Daisy and I will meet at the top of the Eiffel Tower.

I haven't sent the email yet, but I've pictured how I'll walk up to her, how she'll see me there, ready, finally, and how I will hold her hands and ask her to marry me. James is trying to see if we can get the proposal spelled out in lights at the bottom of the Tower.

And after she says yes, I'll throw in, "Oh, and can you be the Queen of a country, too?"

James and I had agreed I couldn't lead with that.

So, my spirits are high, and I'm feeling pretty positive when I answer the phone.

But my smile fades as I hear the sound of a too-familiar voice.

Leif.

My stomach twists. What could he possibly want? Maybe he's calling to lecture me again, warn me of this whole thing as he did before. I almost ignore it, but I know my brother too well. He won't give up.

I take a deep breath and answer. "Leif."

His voice is cold, almost venomous. "Look outside your door."

Before I can react, I hear footsteps outside, and my heart races. I unlock the door just as Leif steps inside, his gaze cutting through me like a blade.

James, who'd been tapping away on his laptop, straightens. I feel his eyes watching us carefully. We've both seen Leif in this mood before. It's never pretty.

Leif steps closer, crossing his arms. "Do you know a beautiful American girl with dark skin and a heart too big for her own good?"

I feel the blood drain from my face. "What . . . Leif, what are you talking about?"

"Oh, come on, Leo. You know exactly who I mean. Don't even pretend."

My heart pounds. "Just tell me what happened. Leave nothing out."

Leif's eyes narrow. "Daisy knows."

Every nerve in my body freezes. "Knows . . . what?"

"Everything, Leo." His words drop like lead, heavy and cutting. "The truth. The whole damn truth. Whatever twisted hide-and-seek game you've been playing with her mind is over."

I stumble back a step, but Leif's glare keeps me pinned. James stands up, ready for whatever happens next.

I can barely breathe, my mind spiraling, trying to make sense of what Leif is saying.

"I never meant—"

"No?" Leif's voice sharpens, the word dripping with disdain. "You never meant for her to discover you're here in Paris after ghosting her? You never meant to tell her you have a twin who attends her university? You never meant to hurt her? Take your pick."

His words hit like a slap, sharp and scalding, and I feel my chest tighten, as the reality of what he's saying sinks in.

"What . . . did she say?"

"What could she say?" Leif snaps, his voice filled with bitterness. "She was hurt. Betrayed. She thought you were someone else entirely, Leo. And when she realized she was in love with a lie . . . ." He lets the words hang, twisting the knife.

"I have to go see her," I say as calmly as I can, given that my heart is imploding. "To explain. I didn't mean for it to be like this. I was going to ask her to marry me."

From my experience, Leif makes things sound as bad as possible. He's a real drama maker. It's up to me to keep calm and focus on a solution.

Leif laughs bitterly. "So, what's your plan, then? Show up out of the blue, sweep her off her feet, and hope she'll accept that you're the Crown Prince? Then she'll laugh it off as a grand adventure?"

I can't answer him. Every word he's saying, every accusation, is a truth I've been trying to avoid. I glance over at James, who meets my gaze but doesn't say anything, his face unreadable.

As much as I don't want Leif in my affairs, I have to ask, "What did she say when you told her we are the royal family of Arandel?"

The look on Leif's face could freeze ice. "She doesn't even know *that*?" he spits out.

I shake my head. "Didn't you tell her?"

"Damn," he says, "it's worse than I thought. Nope. I didn't think I had to tell her that. She has no idea who you are, does she?"

I stay silent. Not as a sign of power, which silence can be, but out of shame.

Leif shakes his head, his voice quieter but no less intense. "I don't know her very well, but Daisy deserves better, Leo. She deserves someone who isn't playing games with her heart."

"I never did that," I say firmly.

"What do you call ghosting her then?"

I feel the weight of his words pressing down on me, crushing, relentless. And it's clear now that I've hurt her.

"Is she . . . okay?" I ask, my voice breaking.

Leif's gaze softens for the briefest second, but his anger resurfaces. "I have no idea. She was crying her eyes out. Even the strongest people can break."

"Maybe I don't deserve her," I whisper, the admission painful and raw.

Leif gives a short nod. "You're right. You don't."

Without another word, he turns on his heel. The door clicks shut, and the air in the room feels heavier than ever.

James steps forward, his voice commanding. "Leo, we have to accept some defeats. But we stick to the goal."

I shake my head, my throat too tight to speak. There's only one thought in my mind, relentless, unyielding.

I can't fix this. I've already lost her.

Chapter Forty-Four

DAISY

I stare blankly at the ceiling, burrowing under my covers, feeling for the first time that love may not be worth the trouble of finding it.

What a fraud I am! The keeper of love stories, not believing in love.

My breath catches in my throat. I've been crying for the past two days. My eyes are red and raw, my throat itchy and dry.

Without realizing it, I've been asking, "Mom, what do I do?" hoping she'll answer me somehow.

"Any sign would help," I whisper to the spirit of my deceased mom.

If my phone didn't tell me today is Saturday, I wouldn't know or care.

I feel so tired. I haven't slept properly since the evening at school when Leif told me the truth.

My heart is so raw it feels bruised, and food, water, fresh air—none of it matters. All I can do is lie here, scrolling back through photos of us. They're all I have left, and even they feel like they're slipping through my fingers, turning into something less real with every swipe.

My phone screen is covered in fingerprints, and the creases on my face sting where I slept with it pressed against my cheek.

Without knocking, Lulu bursts into my room, marching like she's about to tackle a wild beast. "Okay, enough," she says, yanking open the curtains.

Sunlight pours unrelenting beams into my room, making me wince.

"Lulu, please—" I start, my voice hoarse.

"Nope," she interrupts, crossing her arms. "You're not staying in bed all day, wallowing. I know you're hurt. Believe me, I get it. But moping around isn't going to change anything. Now, go wash up. Today, you're not allowed to feel sorry for yourself."

I sit up slowly, my head pounding. "How am I supposed to face the world? Or even leave the apartment?"

"Catch," Lulu says, tossing a doll into my hands.

"What's this?" I ask, inspecting it. The doll has seen better days —black soot stains smudge its fabric, and someone's drawn green stripes across it with a marker.

"That's Lulu. The original Lulu."

I frown. "I'm not following."

Lulu leans against my dresser, crossing her arms. "Years ago, when I first came to France, I was all alone and barely understood the French everyone spoke. It felt different here. Everything was different. I was so homesick I wanted to catch the next boat or plane home. But my family needed me; I was their lifeline to a better future. So I swallowed my heartache and got to work."

She glances at the doll in my hands. "About a week later I had a turning-point conversation with my family, reminding me of the difficult life they had back home. That's when I found that doll. She had 'Lulu' sewn on her collar, so that's what I called her."

The doll's stitching is frayed, her clothes worn thin. Lulu laughs softly. "She needed a dress, or pants, or anything to cover her. And even though I asked around, no one claimed her. She was just there, like a reminder—a reminder to stop spiraling and find something to hold on to."

I look down at the doll, realizing how much meaning it must carry for her. Lulu takes a breath. "An immigration officer, the woman processing my papers, told me something I'll never forget: 'Start with small steps, and don't expect everything to be how you imagined it.' She was right. And I did. One step at a time, like we'll do today."

She straightens up, giving me an encouraging look. "Now, how about a shower? Then we're getting out of here."

When I don't move, she grabs my hand, pulling me up with her natural strength. "I know you're a wet noodle right now, Dais, but that's not who you are. Remember your mission?"

I look at her, confused.

"The locks, Daisy," she says, as if this should be obvious. "All the couples who messaged you, waiting for you to help them find their love stories. These people believe in love, just like you do."

"Did," I blurt.

Lulu side-eyes me. "If you're well enough to talk back, you're well enough to . . . *you know*?"

"Fix love? Like I'm a love repair person?"

"You don't wear sarcasm well."

"Sorry," I mumble.

It feels strange to think about those messages now with my mind still fogged with heartbreak.

But Lulu's eyes are so fierce that, somehow, I find myself nodding. I head to the bathroom, letting the hot water run over me as I try to shake off the numbness.

When I look at myself in the mirror, red-rimmed eyes and all, I feel a glimmer of determination.

Lulu's right. There's something I can still hold onto, something real. Even if my own love story is crumbling, I still have other people to bring together.

Twenty minutes later, I'm dressed and ready, or at least as close to ready as I'll get. Lulu hands me a cup of strong coffee, giving me a quick, satisfied nod as she grabs her bag. "We're doing this."

Lulu and I walk out the door together, her hand firmly gripping my arm.

"I'm not one of your little dolls, you know."

A glittery lip gloss smile lights up Lulu's face. "Darling, you wish."

The edges of my lips slide up a tiny bit as we hit the pavement of Paris on the sunny fall day.

"Thanks, Mom," I whisper, recognizing the signs all around me.

Chapter Forty-Five

DAISY

The metallic *snip, snip, snip* echoes across the bridge as Lulu and I approach.

Each lock is being cut and tossed into a large bin with a harsh finality.

Watching them pile up, each one a memory, a promise, it's almost too much. I can't help the tears welling up.

"Oh, no," Lulu murmurs beside me. "Daisy, if you cry, we'll all be a mess here. We have to get to work."

I sniff, nodding.

"I know, Lulu. It's just—look at them." I motion to the locks, scattered and broken, discarded as if they didn't hold entire love stories inside.

"Well, we'll fix it, won't we?" Lulu says, rolling up her sleeves like she's ready to battle the entire world. She nudges me. "And hey, don't forget your own words—you're preserving love here, not giving it up. So, come on."

Feeling slightly more focused, I start snapping photos of the locks on a little cloth I've spread out on the bridge, logging each one for the virtual bridge I created online.

I type out a message and post it, hoping the world will understand what's happening here:

"If you ever locked a token of love onto the Pont des Arts in Paris, your lock is being taken down to preserve the bridge. But it's not too late to save your love lock! Tell me about it, share your story, and let's give these symbols of your heart a new home."

I hit "post" and look up just in time to see Maxine approaching, her face flushed and her hair slightly windblown.

I'd messaged her and Étienne on our way to the bridge.

Meet us at the Pont des Arts. Operation Locked in Love is in full effect.

"Don't you dare start without me!" she says, dropping her bag on the ground. "Did you think I'd miss out on the love lock revolution?"

"Of course not." I hug her. "Glad you're here."

"How are you?" Maxine's eyes peer deeper into mine than I'd like. She witnessed my breakdown, and I feel a bit mortified.

As if she picks up on my embarrassment, she says, "Happens to all of us at one time or another. Love makes us crazy."

At that moment, Marc appears, and I introduce them.

Marc's eyes light up talking to Maxine in French, something he couldn't do without a lot of explanations when talking to me.

The two of them are laughing and examining locks together in no time.

Lulu starts humming that song from the movie *Love Actually*, about love being all around. I join in. Tourists stop and snap photos of us with the locks, singing very badly.

I tell anyone who shows interest to post the photos and videos to my IG page.

"Aren't we the little social media marketer?" Lulu teases me. "Use your skills to market love, baby."

As if on cue, Étienne appears right behind Lulu, carrying a box and flashing me a warm smile.

"Couldn't let you do this alone. I brought some supplies—a box for the locks you want to keep, cleaning cloths, and a metal cleanser to get off decades of grime. Thought it might help."

He doesn't say anything about me not answering my phone for two days. For that I am grateful.

"Oh, you're here," Lulu teases. "It's a full-on rescue mission."

She appraises him as he puts down all his gear for cleaning the locks. She raises her eyebrows. "So far, so good."

Étienne smirks, playfully. "I'm happy to impress." He crouches down, carefully picking up a lock and brushing off the dust with a cloth.

"You know, Daisy, what you're doing here is more than a project—it's a gift."

I shrug, half-embarrassed. "It's not that big a deal."

Maxine shakes her head. "It is a big deal, Daisy. If you weren't orchestrating *Save Love Locks*, all these beautiful souvenirs would be lost."

Étienne hands me a lock with two names carefully etched into it, and as I turn it over in my hand, I feel a ray of hope. "Some of these stories deserve to be kept alive. I'll make sure they don't just disappear."

The three of them work with me, helping to clean each lock, organize them, and take more photos.

Étienne carefully dusts each one, Maxine reads out the names engraved on them, and Lulu uses her phone to document the process for the virtual bridge.

Etienne holds up one particularly weathered lock. "Look at this one—fifteen years, maybe? It's more art than metal now."

We take turns admiring the etched hearts and ribbons spelling out the names of *Miguel* and *Pansy* on the lock.

"I wonder where they are. I hope someone sees the photo and writes in." I hear the wistfulness in my tone. As if I wish it were me who this lock belonged to.

Maxine nods in agreement. "Daisy, you've created a community of love lock savers. It's like everyone who ever believed in a fairy tale is finding each other on your social media page, and your new website."

I laugh a little, finally feeling a moment of lightness as I take another photo. "Well, I might as well make my time in Paris count, right?"

I know Maxine and Lulu will understand the meaning of my words. I don't expect Étienne to reach over and place a hand on my shoulder.

"You're doing more than that." His gaze is steady, and for a moment, the sadness I've been carrying feels a little lighter.

The pile of locks grows, and so do the comments and hearts on my posts.

A stream of memories and stories files in as people share stories about having their locks placed on this bridge at some point in their lives.

It's a memory bank growing with love stories.

As each message appears, I feel something inside me start to heal, as if I'm not alone in this journey.

Étienne finishes wiping down a lock and leans back, a contemplative look in his eyes. "You're doing what I could never do," he says quietly. "I paint moments, but they stay frozen on canvas. What you're doing is living art, capturing stories that still have a future."

Lulu nods with a grin. "That's our Daisy, alright. Art with a heart."

I burst out laughing. "Art with a heart. Wait until I tell my sisters. But seriously, thank you, guys. I don't know what I'd do without you all."

At that moment, Jake crosses the bridge and plops down beside us. "I came as soon as I could."

He picks up a lock. "R.J. and Fluffy," he reads the inscription. "And there's a paw print on the back."

We get somber.

I snap a photo of the lock and post it with words I read aloud:

"*Love comes in all shapes, sizes, human and nonhuman, colors, and identities. But the most important thing is to live and love.*"

"Awwww," Lulu says, gripping her heart in a non-sarcastic way. "That's *purrrfect*."

We collapse into laughter and end up singing the *Love Is All Around Us* song as we keep working on the *Locked in Love* project.

It doesn't escape me that I might not have my fairy tale, but with friends like these, maybe I've got something better.

Chapter Forty-Six

LEO

The tension in my chest hasn't eased since Leif left. His words—"You don't deserve her"—keep circling in my mind, an echo that won't let up.

I've been pacing the apartment for hours, aimless, my thoughts as scattered as the leaves falling from the trees outside.

James sighs, glancing up from his phone. "If you don't stop pacing, I might start doing laps around this room myself."

I force a laugh, but even that comes out hollow.

He stands and claps a hand on my shoulder. "Enough. Let's get out of here, man. Get some air, get some perspective. Maybe find you a baguette."

I nod, glad for the distraction, and we head out. We wander down to the Seine. I struggle to let the noise and energy of the city drown out my thoughts.

Then, on a whim, James points to one of the riverboats lining the dock.

"Why not?" he says, grinning. "It's a touristy move, but we're tourists right now, aren't we? At least I am. Let the river carry us away. They serve drinks on board, too," he winks.

I laugh for real this time, and soon we're boarding a *bateaux mouche*, the kind that cruises the Seine, giving passengers an unobstructed view of the city's bridges and famous landmarks.

We settle on the open-air deck. The breeze is blowing cold but the sunshine makes up for the brisk air.

James pretends to shiver violently in his sports jacket.

As the boat pulls away, I feel a sense of relief, the kind that comes from leaving something behind, even if just for an hour.

We stand at the rail, watching the city slide by. Every bridge has its own character, and every building carries the weight of history. As we pass under the first bridge, James nudges me.

"Remember when we used to sneak into the library to read about the other monarchies? You thought you could convince the Queen to change your duties by showing her what other kingdoms do," he laughs.

I roll my eyes. "Yeah, well, I was fourteen. Back then, I thought the world would bend to my will if I argued hard enough."

"Don't give yourself that much credit—you still think that," he teases, and we both laugh.

It's good to have James here, reminding me of where we came from and how far we've come. But still, something gnaws at me. "Do you ever think about what life would be like if we weren't, you know, part of *them*?"

James nods. "I think about how lucky I am. Even if the responsibilities are heavier than we ever signed up for."

We pass the Conciergerie, the medieval fortress and former prison that housed Marie Antoinette before her execution.

"Like that building," I point. "It's the remaining part of the Palais de la Cité, which was the residence and seat of power of the kings of France *in the Middle Ages*. Can you believe that was a monarch's home? There are sacrifices but also so much opulence.

Most of it is unnecessary as that amount of riches for one family takes away from the people's maintenance and survival."

I look out over the water, watching the play of light on the rippling surface. "This heartbreaking disaster with Daisy . . . . It makes me realize we don't just serve ourselves."

James crosses his arms. "You got me on a boat ride to discuss philosophy, Leo. All I can say is when we're the rulers, we can make the changes."

"Agreed," I say, shaking his hand. "Progress is key. If you stand still, you die."

At that moment, the boat is jostled by the current, and we grip the rail to stay on our feet.

We laugh about nature's timing, letting us know she is the ultimate ruler.

The boat's PA system cuts in, announcing the Pont des Arts ahead. My heart jolts, instinctively, and I straighten.

Up on the bridge, I spot a group of people, but they're not tourists. They're clustered together, holding what looks like phone cameras. They're snapping pictures of something they're holding up.

And then I see her.

"James! There!" I grab his arm as I bounce on my feet.

"It's Daisy! She's on the bridge!"

James whistles. "Whoa, wait—are you sure?"

"It's her!" My heart is racing louder than the boat's engine. Without thinking, I'm waving, jumping like an idiot, anything to make sure she sees me.

She turns, her face like an angel against the sky, her hair bundled on top of her head.

My heart swoops right out of my chest.

Her gaze locks onto mine. Her gaze tells me she sees me—Leo of Arandel.

I swear, for just a second, everything feels right again.

But then, in the next heartbeat, she looks away, turning back to her friends holding up small objects that catch the light.

She's back taking photos as if I'm nothing to her. Like I'm just another face in the crowd.

I keep waving, my energy starting to crack as she keeps ignoring me.

James's next to me, his eyes squinting in the sunshine.

"You sure she saw you?"

"She looked right at me, James!" I shout, the frustration mounting. "She knows it's me. She has to."

James's smile fades slightly, and he gives me a serious look. "Or . . . she thinks it's someone else. You know . . . Leif."

I falter, a cold chill settling in my gut. It hadn't occurred to me. After everything Leif said, what if Daisy can't tell us apart anymore? Or worse—what if she doesn't want to?

Chapter Forty-Seven

DAISY

I lean against the railing of the Pont des Arts, trying to focus on anything but him. Leo. Or whoever it was I saw on that boat.

My mind insists it was just another flicker of Paris casting shadows.

My friends are still gathering locks, snapping photos, laughing over stories shared on my page—each of them seems happy, rooted in this moment. Meanwhile, I'm . . . somewhere else.

Étienne catches my eye as I straighten up. He's watching me with that warm, intense gaze, tilting his head as if he can sense that I'm lost in thought.

He comes over and stands by my side.

"You look like you've seen a ghost," he says softly, his dark eyes searching mine.

I swallow and force a smile. "Maybe I have."

He frowns, probably wondering what I mean, but I don't elaborate.

I know I need to clear my head. "I think I'll take a walk," I say, forcing brightness into my voice. "Just need a little breather."

Lulu nods, glancing at me with an understanding look.

"We'll keep things running here. Go on, clear your head. And come back when you're ready."

I smile at her, grateful as always, and turn to slip away from the bridge, from my friends, from all of it.

THE STILLNESS ALONG THE SEINE FEELS GROUNDING, like pressing pause on everything.

I breathe deeply, inhaling the faint scents of river water, wet stone, and autumn leaves, grounding myself in each breath. *It wasn't him,* I repeat, like a mantra.

It couldn't have been.

But the closer I get to the memory, the more real it feels, the way his hair caught the light, his eyes catching mine with that familiar spark . . . .

Then I see him.

Standing a few feet ahead, leaning over the riverbank as if trying to catch his breath.

His hair, windswept and a little wild, his hands gripping his knees as if he's been running for miles. And when he looks up—those eyes, so familiar, pin me in place. Leif looks nothing like Leo. How could I confuse the two?

"Daisy." His voice, raw and a little hoarse, reaches me like an echo from another life.

He straightens, his eyes boring into mine. The intensity is unlike anything I've ever experienced.

I don't move. Part of me wants to turn and run, while another part of me feels rooted to this spot, caught between beautiful memories and the hard reality of now.

Leo steps closer, moving cautiously like he's afraid I'll disappear if he breathes wrong. His expression flickers between hope and something I can't place, something almost vulnerable.

"Daisy," he says again, softer this time. "I . . . I didn't think I'd see you today. I thought you'd . . . ." His voice trails off as he searches my face, looking for something, some reaction.

"I didn't expect to see you at all," I say, my voice tight. "Not here, not anywhere. Not after you—" I stop, the word *left* hanging between us, weighty and unfinished.

He drops his gaze, and when he looks back up, his face is shadowed, his eyes raw.

"I know I don't deserve to stand here, asking for even a second of your time," he says, and his voice cracks a little. "But I need you to know, Daisy, there's nothing in this world I regret more than the way I left."

For a heartbeat, I can't even breathe. I wanted this—an apology, maybe some explanation to fill the void he left. But hearing him say it, watching the pain cross his face, makes the hurt even sharper, not easier.

"You just disappeared, Leo. Like I meant nothing."

My words come out harder than I intended, but they're the truth, and the truth has been bottled up inside me for too long.

"I waited for months. And then I just . . . I had to move on."

He closes his eyes for a moment, breathing in slowly.

"I was scared," he admits, his voice barely above a whisper. "Scared that if I told you who I really am, if I told you everything, you'd . . . you'd run. I know that sounds selfish, and it was. But it's the truth. I wasn't just hiding from you—I was hiding from myself, from everything I knew I couldn't have." He swallows, the pain etched into every line of his face.

My heart tightens. "What do you mean who you really are? Who are you supposed to be?"

"You don't know?" he asks.

"Know what?" I ask exasperated.

"I thought . . . Leif would have said. Or you might have discovered it some other way."

I feel the creases grow in my forehead like a philosophical debate is happening, and I'm clueless.

"Who *are* you?" I ask.

Then, I swallow hard. "No," I raise a hand and press it against the air. "Don't tell me. I am not interested."

I glance at the bridge behind me. "I have a lot of people waiting for me to work on a project of love. It means a lot to me. Let's just say it was nice knowing each other and leave it at that. Because honestly, Leo, I'm not sure our . . . whatever this is . . . is worth all this heartache, when real lovers, with their real love stories, are waiting for me."

Before he can say another word, I turn and hurry off.

I don't look back over my shoulder. I walk as swiftly as I can away from the pain in my heart as if I can outrun it.

I walk away from Leo's hurt eyes (how dare he?!). And I walk away from what could have been my own love story.

Only if.

Chapter Forty-Eight

LEO

"It's over," I say to James, dropping heavily onto the couch.

"What did she say when you told her about, you know . . . being King, the whole needing-to-marry thing, and whether she could be your Queen?"

I shrug, feeling like I'm sinking further into the cushions with each word. "I didn't get a chance to tell her any of that. She still doesn't know I'm the Crown Prince. Leif didn't tell her."

James lets out a low whistle. "So, you two connected, chatted for, what? Ten minutes? And you skipped over the single most important part? That you need her to marry you?"

"'Need' sounds so . . . needy," I mutter, wincing. "I want her to want to marry me."

"Want . . . need, let's call it whatever you want. You don't have time to waste here. Courtship is over, my friend; you're at Step 49 already."

I let out a sharp laugh. "I can't rush her, James."

He smirks. "Well, it seems to me you're failing at basic diplomatic relations. Professor Schultz would be mortified if he knew this is what you took away from his class."

"We need a summit," I mutter, half to myself.

"Better: we need a face to face," James replies, leaning forward.

"Exactly. I have to tell her the most important thing of all."

"That you think the royal cape would look great on her shoulders?"

I roll my eyes. "Seriously, dude?"

"Just adding some levity before I collapse here." He laughs. "You've got me thinking we're doomed."

"Never say die," I reply, clapping his shoulder.

"First rule of power?"

"First rule of love. Where's your mind at? Sheesh!"

James clicks his tongue. "You sure you don't want to just marry a princess from another realm and get this over with so we can play some video games?"

I push James on his shoulder. "Thanks for being here."

He rubs his palms together. "Paving the way for favors from your country to mine."

"Consider it done."

Later, I sit in front of my laptop, scrolling through the posts on Daisy's website.

Reading her words in response to questions about missing locks is as close as I can get to her right now.

My neck aches from bending over my laptop for hours to scroll through her messages. That's when I see a new link.

It leads to the stories Daisy is crafting about locks she discovered on the bridge that seem interesting to her, either the names or initials, the time period, or some message on the locks that catch her eye.

Daisy has created something very special. Something that combines the old, the bridge and locks, with the new, a virtual love museum.

There is a sense of camaraderie amongst the lock lovers who talk about leaving bits of their hearts in Paris.

Some comment that they are still going strong after decades. Some have lost their love to disease, illness, war, or plain mind-numbing divorce.

But they all thank Daisy for bringing them back to the beautiful moments when they clasped their loved ones' hands and sealed their love together in Paris.

I'm mesmerized by Daisy's writing. She captures the love stories of those whose voices are not here.

Ghost loves. Kind of like mine and hers.

I knew Daisy wanted to be a writer, and these stories are a testament not only to her love for love but also to her desire to reach people through her written words.

I'm so proud of her. I want to tell her. I want to hold her in my arms and never let her go.

Seeing her today, she looked more mature, more worldly, so sure of herself and confident in what she's accomplishing.

She would make a fantastic Queen for Arandel, and a challenging, beautiful wife to me.

My fingers itch to tell her how proud I am of her.

But would that be too little too late?

I can compliment her writing, though. I don't have to make this about how I feel—which is proud, but sad—or what I want—which is for her to be mine.

I can make this all about her because even when you lose the one you love, you still want the best for them, right?

I type carefully, deleting often, revising and editing until it's just right:

I think the world would love to see an anthology of these love stories. Your writing is captivating and encouraging for anyone searching for their one and only or who has lost their loved one. Why not combine these stories in a book?

I'm one of these love locks, too. I locked a lock on the bridge for the woman I love, and now it's lost amongst a sea of metal.

My heart feels like it's been clipped like the locks. Severed. I can still see the look in her eyes when she said that whatever we had wasn't worth the heartache.

She wouldn't have said that if she didn't feel something, too. It wasn't just me. Was there a way to resuscitate it?

I stare out the window at the Eiffel Tower just blocks away from my Paris home.

Its iconic shape glows against the night sky. This building, this apartment—my great-grandparents bought it years ago, securing a view of Paris that sweeps across the city's rooftops and captures the tower itself in all its majesty.

Less than a year ago, Daisy stood here with me, looking out at this same view.

Her sister, Corrine, was here too, struggling with her love for a man she thought was not right for her.

While Corrine was lost in her thoughts, Daisy and I shared the small treats we'd picked up that day. French chocolate, aromatic goat cheese, macarons in a rainbow of colors, and a bottle of Crémant—the bubbly wine from the Alsace region.

"The region with the Christmas markets," I'd told her. "I promise we'll go there next Christmas," I'd said, thinking I had all the time in the world.

Back then, my father was in remission. His cancer had been

dormant for two years. He and Mother were content ruling Arandel, while I was free to chase the waves.

I'm learning that time is fleeting, like love.

We always think we have a lot of time. I thought it would be years before I'd have to settle down in Arandel, get married, and be ready to run a country. Not months.

I look back at the Eiffel Tower. On the hour, every hour, its lights go wild. Thousands of golden bulbs flash and sparkle, lighting up the night sky in a way that feels almost like magic.

That night, almost one year ago, Daisy and I watched it together, her drink in hand, her shoulder brushing mine.

I could feel the warmth of her skin next to me, as if the city itself was waiting for something to happen between us. I should have kissed her then.

It's funny—I didn't kiss her, but I felt as if I had. That was the power of being beside her.

We stood in silence, mesmerized by the dancing lights of the Eiffel Tower.

"So beautiful," she finally said, breaking the silence.

I'd looked at her and whispered. "Yes, so beautiful."

She meant the lights. I meant her.

Now, that kiss that never happened still lingers as another ghost of our lost love.

Chapter Forty-Nine

DAISY

I sit with my laptop, a hot cup of tea in my hands, scrolling through my messages on *Locked in Love*. Some grip my heart, and I share them with my followers.

"Dearest Daisy," one begins, *"You don't know us, but our story belongs in Paris. In 2004, I came to Paris on vacation, looking for an escape from my busy life in Osaka. My then-boyfriend had just broken my heart, and I needed a change of scenery to get my head and heart on straight. I never expected that I would meet him—a stranger in Paris, a man who would become my true love."*

As I read through their story, a tender picture unfolds of two people whose lives intersected for the briefest of moments. She was from Japan; he, from Argentina. She describes him as tall, his dark hair catching the late-summer sunlight, his eyes pulled her in from the first hello. They met at a small gallery in Montmartre, admiring the same painting—a sunrise over the Seine.

I picture their days wandering through the streets of Paris, tasting croissants, losing themselves in art, language barriers falling away as they discovered how deeply they connected.

They stayed in touch, writing letters and sending postcards over the years, each piece of paper brimming with affection and longing. The more I read, the more I feel as if I'm peering into a love that was never given the chance it deserved.

And then the part that makes my heart skip a beat:

"On the last night of my stay in Paris, we went to the Pont des Arts. He took a small lock from his pocket, a trinket he had bought on a whim, and scrawled our initials on it. He didn't know if we would ever see each other again, but he locked it to the bridge for us, as if to promise that what we had was real, no matter where life took us."

They each went their separate ways. She went back to Osaka, he to Buenos Aires. They had their careers, their families, the twists and turns of life pulling them in opposite directions. And for twenty years, they forgot about the lock—until now, after seeing my posts.

"We've reconnected, Daisy. And we want to come back to Paris. To see if it's still there. To reclaim that lock that held our love in place for so many years, even when we couldn't."

I close my eyes, imagining what it must be like to walk away from a love that felt so strong for twenty years.

I exhale, my fingers hovering over the keyboard before I begin to type.

"This is the story of Yumi from Osaka and Daniel from Buenos Aires. A love that began with a chance meeting and blossomed in the city of light, a city known for capturing the world's secrets and holding them tightly.

Yumi and Daniel are coming back to Paris, to find the lock that holds their memories and, if luck would have it, to find each other once again.

Their journey reminds us that love, like the lights over the Seine, never truly fades. Sometimes, it's just waiting for us to come back."

As I finish typing, a sense of warmth fills me. This city doesn't just belong to the people who live here; it belongs to everyone who's ever loved here.

And maybe, love deserves second chances—if we're brave enough to risk our hearts.

Chapter Fifty

DAISY

October comes and goes, with my classes getting increasingly complex and taking up more and more of my time.

I thought I'd be able to get a part-time job, but between classes, homework, and editing the Anthology of *Locked in Love,* an idea I got from an anonymous comment on my website, the days are full and mostly satisfying.

I'm too busy to think about Leo.

Lulu says I'm keeping busy, so I *don't* think about him.

"You know what they say about things we try to avoid?" Lulu said one day.

I was sitting on the balcony, revising a story for the Anthology that I planned on self-publishing and selling on the website—turning the project into my part-time job.

Every once in a while, I wish I could thank the person who suggested this idea. It is fun, practical, and rewarding all at once.

"What?" I asked, absentmindedly.

"Whatever you push away, you bring closer to you. Right to your doorstep!"

I huff. "I'll take that chance. I doubt Leo Montclair or whatever his name is will show up on our doorstep."

Saying his name out loud made me angry and sad. Like my head and heart were fighting each other over that man.

At school, if I ever glimpsed a tall, lanky, blond-haired guy with a purposeful walk, I headed in the opposite direction.

I figure it's better to be safe than sorry. Who needs to run into a guy who isn't an ex but feels like one?

Anyway, I didn't have *time* to miss Leo. Not anymore.

In the little free time I had, I hung out with Lulu as she sketched designs for her beautiful doll clothes, shopped for the fabric, and created the outfits.

Once the doll company she worked for approved it, the doll and doll clothes patterns were sent to a toy factory.

I'm always amazed whenever Lulu brings home one of the finished prototypes dressed in one of her creations.

Lulu would examine the doll's clothes with a critical eye but then burst into a smile and exclaim, "I can't believe they pay me to do this."

And I'd agree again. "You play with dolls for a living. You're so cool."

The best part was that we'd take photos of the doll in poses around the balcony. Once the doll was released on the market, Lulu packed the prototype securely to mail to her mother in Senegal.

It was an agreement she had with the company. Her mother sold the prototypes, and that money carried the family for a long time.

"It's a doll eat doll's world out there," I teased.

I did get to keep one of the dolls. It was the fairytale princess dressed in a gorgeous white gown with a fur cape and silver heels.

"Your fairytale doll, " Lulu said when she presented it to me.

"I'm not crying," I sniffed as I hugged the beautiful doll.

When I wasn't with Lulu, I went on scooter tours of Paris with Jake, who, despite his cowboy looks and sexy Southern accent, didn't have time to date.

He gave off friend-zone vibes, which were fine with me because I was dating Étienne. Mainly coffee study dates.

When the light outside met Étienne's approval, he'd paint me in front of various Paris buildings. I enjoyed standing or sitting and people-watching while he sketched. And I felt I was contributing to art, a true honor.

So, I had NO time to think about Leo.

This was funny because he was the first thing that popped into my head when I woke up and the last thing I saw in my mind before I fell asleep.

Not to mention, Leo had a starring role in every one of my dreams.

If I thought he had ghosted me by disappearing from my life, now he was the ghost that wouldn't leave me alone.

Chapter Fifty-One

DAISY

The morning is cloudy as Étienne and I make our way to the Pont des Arts bridge, bundled up against the brisk October air. The dampness makes the bridge seem more solemn than usual, almost as if it's feeling the loss of its locks as much as I am.

Étienne and I are quiet as we approach Marc, who waves from the edge, sorting through the day's collected locks in a neat pile by his side.

"You sure you're up for this?" Étienne asks. After weeks together, Étienne and I are no closer physically or emotionally than when we started dating.

It worries me that I'm not feeling that special connection I had with Leo.

Étienne thinks I need time. He said we'd work through it together. I'm grateful for his patience, a virtue I never had.

Now, my gaze fixes on the scattered locks glinting under the gray sky.

"Yes. I want to help Marc with the last of them before class."

Étienne gives me an understanding smile, but I see a hint of uncertainty in his eyes. There's something he can't quite grasp about my connection to this bridge and the locks.

Marc greets us with a nod, brushing a hand through his dark hair. "Morning, you two. I appreciate the help. Just a few more left here before we're done."

Étienne and I join him, quietly sifting through locks, some rusty, some freshly painted. We work side by side, separating out the ones where we can still see the inscriptions from ones too decayed to decipher.

As we reach the last section, I spot one lock dangling off the side, twisted at an odd angle and hanging precariously over the water.

"Oh, look at that," I say, reaching out but coming up short. "It's just out of reach."

Étienne tries next, but even his long arms don't reach it. "Stubborn little thing, isn't it?" he says, glancing at me with a teasing smile. "Looks like it doesn't want to be taken down."

Marc steps forward with his hook, expertly nudging the lock toward us. "I've got it."

As he holds it out to me, I see his face change. "I think this one is for you, Daisy."

"Me? I never put a lock here."

Confused, I take the lock from him. My eyes fall on the neatly engraved words. *Leo loves Daisy.* The letters are surrounded by tiny hearts. I turn it over, my hands trembling. On the back, there's a small daisy etched carefully, and beneath it, the word *Forever.*

For a moment, the world goes silent. My heart hammers in my chest, each beat loud and insistent. *Leo loves Daisy. Forever.*

When did he put this here?

I feel Étienne's gaze on me. There is concern in his eyes and also something else.

"Are you alright?"

I try to nod, but the lump in my throat makes it impossible.

My eyes flicker over the lock again, tracing each letter, as if memorizing every mark, every scratch.

The word *Forever* seems to pierce right through me, a reminder of the promises Leo and I had shared.

Étienne's hand moves to my shoulder, steadying me, but I feel myself slipping away even as he tries to pull me back to the present.

I'd wanted so badly to feel something similar with Étienne, something real and deep and meaningful.

But holding Leo's lock in my hands, I realize how strong the connection with him is.

Marc speaks up. "Daisy, I think you should know . . . . A tall, blond young man left that here for you. About a month ago. He asked me to make sure you'd see it. He seemed . . . serious about it. I'm sorry I didn't tell you. I didn't think he knew you well, so I forgot about it."

"A month?" I whisper in total disbelief.

My mind races, trying to piece together the timeline, to understand why Leo would leave this message and never follow up.

I glance at Étienne. His face is closed off. Like he knows.

I squeeze the lock tightly in my palm, feeling its cold metal press into my skin, anchoring me in a bittersweet truth.

"Maybe this is a sign," I murmur to myself, but both Marc and Étienne hear it.

Étienne's face tightens slightly, but he forces a small, supportive smile. "A sign of what?"

I swallow hard, my heart heavy with the weight of my own words. "That sometimes . . . even when you try to let go, some things—some people—are meant to be in your life."

I can't help the tear that slips down my cheek as I gaze out over the river, the lock still clutched in my hand.

The sun breaks through the clouds just then as if trying to show me some clarity.

I close my eyes, letting the warmth of it seep in. Letting myself feel the love Leo left here for me.

Étienne says nothing, but I feel the quiet acceptance in his expression, a silent acknowledgment that he knows, maybe even has always known, that some things can't be forced, no matter how much you want them.

I take a shaky breath, whispering a thank you to both of them, and as I slip the lock into my pocket, I feel something settle deep inside me—alongside a familiar pang of uncertainty.

And for the first time in weeks, I wonder, *Is my story with Leo really over? Or just beginning?*

Whether I'm ready or not, it's time for some answers.

Chapter Fifty-Two

LEO

James stands by the doorway, his bags packed and ready to go. He's been summoned to attend some diplomatic affairs back home.

I was lucky to have him by my side for as long as I did.

He's dressed casually, but there's an air of purpose around him, the way he looks when he's preparing for something big, like a tournament or one of his diplomatic outings.

"So this is it," he says, watching me with that assessing gaze he's had since we were kids. "Time to stop running around Paris, Leo."

"Feels like it," I say, the words heavier than I expected.

James sighs, leaning his back against the door frame. "Listen, just because we're used to getting what we want doesn't mean it's always meant for us."

He lets his words settle before speaking again.

"In Zulu culture, there's an old story. A young man—powerful, clever—spent years chasing something beautiful and fleeting, thinking it would bring him the happiness he'd dreamed of. But every time he got close, it slipped through his fingers. He didn't realize it wasn't his to claim, but his to learn from."

He pauses, searching my face. "And when he finally let go, he became wise. Strong. The kind of man people would follow."

I try to take it in, but it's a bitter truth to swallow. "So what are you saying?" I ask, a half-hearted laugh escaping me. "That Daisy isn't mine?"

James puts a hand on my shoulder. "Maybe she's meant to be, maybe not. That's something only you'll know when you're not chasing her. Leo, we're future leaders. We can't let the world slip away from us while we obsess over one thing, one person."

He lets out a deep breath, eyes softening as he continues. "Sometimes the best thing you can do, if you truly care, is to let them go. Let them be free, without the shadow of us always behind them."

His words twist around my heart, tightening and loosening at the same time. "Let her go?" I echo, barely hearing my own voice.

James nods, his hand leaving my shoulder. "Look, you made a mistake, and it's eating you up. That's okay. We all mess up. But it's how we learn. You don't want to be haunted by this, Leo. Leave Paris, go back to Arandel. Let her find what's right for her."

I give him a hard nod, knowing deep down that he's right. My mind is buzzing with the thought of it, with the pain of letting her go—but also a strange kind of release.

"Let's go home," James says, his voice low. "You to Arandel. Me to South Africa. We both have responsibilities waiting for us."

We shake hands, and it's like a final seal on his words, on this chapter of my life.

After he's gone, I call Leif and leave a message. "I'm heading back. If you want the apartment, it's all yours."

I grab my coat and walk through the city one last time, heading toward the bridge. When I reach the Pont des Arts, the cool air brings a sense of finality. I spot her almost instantly.

Daisy is there, wrapped up in a coat and a pink beanie. Her dark curls tumble around her face.

She's hugging someone, a man . . . the artist guy she's been going out with.

She's clinging to him, her fingers pressed into his jacket like he's an anchor. And his arms wrap around her in a way that tells me everything.

I close my eyes to block out the scene. That should be me. If Daisy needs to hold on to someone for any reason, it should be to me.

James's words reverberate in my mind.

I can't intrude on her happiness. I can't disrupt what I've already hurt.

I force a smile on my face, and a bittersweet acceptance in my heart. She deserves this. Deserves happiness, peace, and someone who won't let her down.

"I'm happy for you, Daisy," I whisper to myself, like a gentle farewell. *The beautiful princess of my heart.*

And with that, I turn and walk away. An empty feeling in my soul that may never be filled.

Kingdom of Arandel

Chapter Fifty-Three

DAISY

It's just me.

Alone in Paris for the first time—no sisters, no Leo, no Lulu, no Jake, no Étienne. Just me.

It's amazing what you notice when you're alone, like the ancient gargoyles perched high on buildings, their twisted, contorted faces watching as I walk through the streets.

They've seen it all: war and peace, love and heartbreak, triumph and tragedy. Beautiful Paris, city of light.

So much beauty, hidden in plain sight.

I marvel at the tiny ornate balconies, wrought-iron railings curling in delicate designs that look like lace against the old stone.

Boulangeries display rows of brightly colored macarons in their gleaming windows, each one a bite-sized masterpiece stacked in elaborate pyramids.

I nibble on flaky croissants that nearly bring me to tears with their light, buttery layers. Crêpes sizzle, their edges caramelized and alight with flambéed brandy in the twilight.

I walk and walk, winding my way through neighborhoods, losing myself in the shifting character of each arrondissement.

I eventually reach the highest point of the city, where the streets are alive with voices speaking a dozen dialects.

Little Africa, where fabric stores line the streets and seamstresses work magic behind the windows, dressing men and women in vibrant patterns that seem to float like magic carpets.

Paris, diverse and ever-changing, unfolds like a tapestry.

I pass Nelson Mandela Park, where children's laughter mixes with lively conversations.

I wander through Père Lachaise Cemetery, pausing before the graves of Jim Morrison and Oscar Wilde, feeling the weight of art and rebellion in the air.

I stand in front of the Moulin Rouge, its iconic red windmill spinning slowly, and imagine Paris in the roaring 1920s, alive with jazz and champagne and a kind of joy that feels timeless.

I linger on the steps of the Basilica of Sacré-Cœur, its gleaming white towers looking like a fairytale castle.

As I move, I pass parks with carousels where parents sit on benches watching their children ride the painted horses.

Street musicians play their instruments better than concerts you buy tickets to attend.

I stare into ponds that mirror the golden leaves clinging to the tree branches, not ready to let go and drift to the ground.

I find myself wandering for hours in the Luxembourg Gardens. The gardens were created in the early 1600s as a place of beauty, and later, it was where Parisians demonstrated, discussed political ideas, and expressed themselves freely.

I perch on the edge of one of many chairs in the gardens, mesmerized by the ornate Italian-styled Medici Fountain and its statue of the giant one-eyed Cyclops, Polyphemus. In front of the giant are statutes of lovers Acis and Galatea.

Polyphemus was in love with Galatea and killed her lover, Acis.

Of all the myths they could have depicted in this serene garden, they chose a dark, violent love.

I get it; love doesn't always work out.

I walk the tree-edged promenades, admiring the chestnut trees on parade, with their leaves changing colors.

Fish and duck ponds, statues, palms, and flower beds are everywhere. Even in the cool weather, the colors are vibrant and alive.

A true oasis in the middle of Paris. I think that, other than the bridges, this garden is my favorite part of the city.

I walk along the pathways, where women walked with frilly parasols centuries ago, the sound of gravel crunching beneath my feet. Did they have love problems back then, too?

Of course, where there are people, there is love.

It feels like Paris itself is speaking to me, finally saying, *Look at me. Look at all I am. I've been waiting for you, Daisy Walker. You've been so wrapped up in other people's love stories that you forgot to live your own.*

For days, I wander around Paris's streets, leaving my scooter parked. I want to feel Paris in my bones, step by step.

I lose myself in the Musée d'Orsay, its vast rooms filled with works by Van Gogh, Monet, and Degas.

I spend an entire day at the Louvre, wandering the large rooms spellbound at the art spilling out everywhere, from tomb walls to the Mona Lisa's tiny frame.

I stand spellbound before the Venus de Milo, her marble form imperfect and powerful.

The goddess of love, Aphrodite herself, gazes back at me with that timeless expression as if to say, *Never give up on love; it's the only reason we are here on earth.*

I imagine that is what the Goddess of Love would say.

Days pass. It's November. School is a blur of faces and facts, but it feels like my real education is happening out here, on the streets of this city, where every corner pulses with history, light, and life.

Paris, you're giving me a new life.

And finally, after weeks of walking through gardens, museums, cemeteries, and neighborhoods, I step back into the Sorbonne with a new clarity and just one thought:

I must find Leif. I must find Leo's brother.

Chapter Fifty-Four

LEO

I throw myself into managing Arandel, trying to ease the weight on my mother's shoulders.

I ride on horseback through the towns and villages of the kingdom with a small entourage that insists on following me, as their future King.

I miss the days when Leif and I would duck them and ride off into the woods, swim in the river, and forage for food in the forest.

The kingdom is surrounded by the Baltic Sea on one side, mountains on another, and a river on the third. It's a veritable fortress with good ports, great seafood, and natural resources.

As the days pass, I feel both busy and healthy from the cold, countryside air. I've stopped dwelling on what I can't have and focus on what I do have.

James is right. If a relationship with Daisy is meant for me, it will be for me.

Meanwhile, I am falling in love with my kingdom in a way I never have before. This would be a wonderful place to raise children, have big furry dogs running around, and enjoy a large family Christmas.

It's not that I've forgotten about Daisy. I am giving my heart a chance to love something else in my life. A feat I do not take for granted given that I will be King one day. One day that is coming far too soon.

I must love the land and Arandel's people to help us all live prosperously.

One evening, as I'm lost in thought, my phone rings, a number I don't recognize flashing on the screen. I hesitate, then answer, "Hello?"

The voice is familiar, though I haven't heard it since that terrible day in Paris.

"Leo. It's me."

"Leif?" I sit up, surprised. "I wasn't expecting your call."

There's a pause. "I imagine not." His tone is tight, restrained. "I heard about the ball. The grand production, you might call it. I suppose you're already getting ready to pick yourself a queen?"

His words are edged, but something sounds off, even for Leif. "It's . . . yes, it's what Father and Mother want."

There's a beat of silence, and then Leif sighs. "This isn't about the ball, Leo. I called about something else. Something you should know."

My stomach tightens. I know my brother well enough to sense there's something personal in this. "Go on."

"She came to see me. Daisy. She found me at the Sorbonne."

I'm stunned. "Daisy came to see you? Why?"

"She had your lock. The one you apparently left on the bridge. She showed it to me herself. She's been carrying it around. She wanted to know how you're doing."

Hearing Daisy's name, the thought of her still holding on to that lock—it's like a knife twisting. "Leif, why are you telling me this?"

He exhales loudly as if this conversation is hard. "Because if it were me, I'd want to know. She wants to talk to you, Leo, and . . . well, whatever grudge I hold isn't enough to keep you from this."

"What does that mean?"

"I don't hate you, Leo. I just wish . . . I wish for once I could be the son they think of first. Neither of our parents has called me to ask if I'm coming to the ball. It's all for you."

"Leif . . . ." I start, but the words fail me. My throat feels tight.

"I know." He cuts me off, his voice resigned. "Listen, do what you want with this information. If you're as caught up with your duty as you say, then maybe you've already moved on from her. But if you haven't . . . ." He trails off, letting me fill in the blanks myself.

I close my eyes, my mind spinning with thoughts of Daisy, of what it would mean to see her again, to explain everything. "Thank you, Leif."

Then I remember something important. "Hey, did you tell her about us?"

"Us?"

"Being princes of Arandel."

"No." Leif's voice crackles through the line, his tone edged with curiosity. "Wait, you're telling me she still doesn't know you're the Crown Prince? Not even a hint?"

I press the phone closer to my ear, pacing the room. "I was going to tell her, Leif. Really. But everything happened so fast, and I couldn't find the right moment. Then she was gone . . . ."

There's a brief silence before he replies, doubt lacing his words. "And she never figured it out? I mean, how has she not Googled you?"

"She follows me on Instagram—my private account. But other than that, I doubt she's gone looking. She's got a lot going on with her classes, her project, her friends . . . ."

Leif laughs, a bit skeptical. "Still, it's strange. You're not exactly an average Joe, Leo. You're all over every royal watch list. The paparazzi call you the Surf King."

"Well, I've stayed out of the public eye for the past year. Incognito, remember?"

"You want me to tell her for you?"

I sigh. "No. She deserves to hear it from me. I need to be the one to tell her."

"Well," Leif says, "Better make it soon. She's looking for answers."

The line goes silent, and then he's gone.

I set my phone down, my pulse racing. The thought of Daisy searching for me stirs something in me I can't ignore, a pull as fierce as gravity itself.

Chapter Fifty-Five

DAISY

I stare at my screen, waiting for the call to connect, fingers fidgeting nervously. Seconds later, my sisters' faces pop up, framed in different backgrounds—Emerald's overlooking a grey ocean, Ava in front of a glass case filled with gelato, Corrine on a sunny beach and Bridget perched outside, her hair whipping wildly in the wind.

Lulu is squeezed in next to me on our tiny couch, leaning her head on my shoulder with a grin as she waves.

"Hey, Lulu!" Ava calls, laughing as if they've all known each other forever. It's grounding, having them here, even virtually, and Lulu by my side.

"So, what's this 'urgent' thing that needed a family meeting?" Emerald asks, eyebrows arched, already anticipating some dramatic twist.

"Don't tell me you and Lulu have started a side business," Bridget teases.

Lulu snickers. "Nah, not yet. But I see a diverse line of dolls in love coming soon."

My sisters laugh, and I feel a little of the tension dissolve.

But then I take a breath and say, "I ran into Leo's twin brother, Leif, here in Paris."

There's a collective intake of breath on the other end, with reactions ranging from Emerald's wide-eyed gasp, Ava's stunned silence, and Bridget's muffled laughter as she chokes on her coffee.

"Leo has a twin?!" Corrine shouts. She's the only sister to meet Leo. In fact, she introduced us.

I nod. "I know! None of us knew. And get this," I say, leaning in conspiratorially, "he told me there's something about Leo I need to hear . . . from Leo himself."

They stare at me, slack-jawed, before Bridget raises her glass in mock solemnity. "I'd like to toast to the most mysterious and dramatic romantic entanglement I've ever heard. Secret twin brother, now another secret. "

"You have to admit, Daisy, this sounds like the plot of a romance novel," Emerald says, her eyebrows lifted. "Right up your alley."

I roll my eyes. "Emerald, this is *my* real life."

Emerald grins and shrugs. "Sometimes life out-romances fiction. So, what did Leif say?"

I sigh, leaning back. "Not much. Just that if I want to know the whole story, I'd need to ask Leo myself. There's a secret Leo hasn't told me."

"A secret?" Ava raises her eyebrows, intrigued. "So now you have to hunt him down?"

"Feels like it," I mutter. "Except I'm not sure if I want to know what it is. I mean, what if it's something . . . unforgivable?"

Lulu speaks to the crowd. "I think Daisy's more scared of the truth than of losing him."

Bridget's face is filled with sympathy. "Daisy, I don't think you'd be so torn up if you didn't really want to know the truth. I think you're trying to protect yourself. Which I get . . . but doesn't sound very 'Daisy,' if you ask me. You are fearless."

"Me?"

Emerald jumps in. "Yes, you. You flew across the ocean for a semester in Paris, all in the name of independence. Now look at you, tangled up in romance and secrets. You've come too far to back down now, honey."

"Is that advice?" I ask, smiling despite myself.

"It's practically a command." Emerald grins.

Ava clears her throat, cutting in. "I think the question is whether you want the fairy tale or reality. Fairy tales . . . they're wonderful, but maybe this one is about finding out if a real guy, with flaws and imperfections, can still be your prince."

Lulu claps her hands over her head. "Amen."

The girls laugh, but I feel my heart beat faster. "If only it were that simple," I say, my voice small.

Emerald gives me a serious look. "Daisy, I know you're scared. But do you want to let fear decide this for you?"

I bite my lip, feeling torn. "It's just . . . it feels too big. I can't shake the feeling there's something huge he hasn't told me. What if it changes everything?"

Emerald leans in close to the screen. "This could be your 'happily ever after' moment, but you must take the risk."

"I don't know if I'm brave enough for all this," I whisper, feeling a swell of emotions.

Emerald's face fills the screen. "Daisy, you're braver than anyone I know. Go get your fairy tale, whatever that looks like."

I close my eyes, feeling the truth of her words settle in my heart. "Alright," I say quietly, "I'll do it."

Lulu whoops beside me, giving me a gentle push. "There's our Daisy. Now, let's get some pastries and plan this out. No grand mission should be done on an empty stomach."

"You're so one of us," Ava laughs. Corrine and Bridget agree. "Welcome to the family, Lulu."

Lulu looks like she might cry.

My support group is overflowing with love, the kind you keep forever.

It makes what's coming next a little bit easier to face.

Chapter Fifty-Six

LEO

Seeing Father so peaceful in the garden surrounded by tall green cypress trees, my heart goes out to him. I don't want to be the one to disturb his peace, but I must tell him about Leif's phone call.

If anything can or will be done, it needs to be now. There is no more later.

"Leif called," I start, after he invites me to sit with him.

"He told me Daisy came to him looking for me. But he was hurt, Father. He resents me and feels like he's always been overshadowed by the fact that I'll be King. It feels as if he's spent his whole life waiting to step into a role that doesn't quite belong to him."

Father sighs, a deep sadness filling his gaze. "I suppose there's always been a shadow cast, however unintentionally." He looks out over the garden.

"Leif wants to be more than an extra heir," I challenge. "Can't we do something about that?"

"We never wanted him to feel lesser than you or anyone,"

Father says. "But what he wants . . . to be King . . . it won't happen."

"He might not want to be the actual *King*," I suggest. "But he wants a role as close as possible, something to make his mark. I never realized how much my position has cost him."

Father's expression softens, and he nods. "I'll speak to Leif. He deserves the chance to feel that he is valued here, that he has a place in the kingdom beyond simply 'Prince Leif.' We'll find a way for him to serve Arandel in a way that honors his talents and ambitions."

He chuckles lightly, "Perhaps he'll even find a bride of his own at the ball. He can dance with all our guests since you are so enamored with just one."

I grin, imagining Leif fending off women, and men, longing to be close to him. "Please, save him from that if you can."

Father grins, "Why? Leif might love it."

We have a small laugh. I try not to let Father talk too much. He ends up coughing and spitting out nothing.

But he seems excited to welcome Leif home and throw the royal ball.

And if we can close the riff between me and Leif, the ball would be well worth it.

"May both Princes find their partners at the ball," says Father with a wink.

"I'm bringing a date," I say, hoping against hope that it will be Daisy Walker.

"You do that, son," Father says. "A King never gives up a valid purpose. But a fool pursues without rhyme or reason."

"I'll try to remember that, Father."

Kingdom of Arandel

Chapter Fifty-Seven

DAISY

The hum of conversation fills the lecture hall as Maxine and I settle into our seats for European History. She's buzzing with excitement, practically bouncing beside me.

"So," she whispers, "I was thinking . . . how about the South of France next weekend?"

I raise an eyebrow, intrigued. "South of France?"

"Yes! The Roman road we've been talking about in class? It's only a train ride away. And we can get some sunshine, maybe explore a vineyard or two." She grins, eyes bright with anticipation.

"I already checked tickets—we could leave Friday afternoon and be back Monday. Just in time to make it back for classes. And we'll stay in this little town called Arles—there's a Roman amphitheater there!" Her enthusiasm is contagious.

"Little town called Arles?" I hoot. "You mean Vincent Van Gogh's preeminent painting site where he painted many of his most beautiful works. I'm in."

Maxine grins. "Yeah, we can do a walking tour of the exact spots he painted from. See the scene from his eye view."

I shake my head at the brilliance of this plan. "You had me at sunshine."

Maxine laughs a little too loudly. Other students give us the evil side eye.

Just as the professor begins his lecture, my phone pings with a new message. I glance down, expecting it to be from one of my sisters, but it isn't. I don't recognize the number.

I frown, reading the message.

Some people hide behind masks, Daisy. I have something to tell you. Please meet me at the top of the Eiffel Tower tonight at 10 p.m. It's urgent.

I show it to Maxine. Her eyes widen. "Ooooh, mystery alert!" she whispers. "Who is it from?"

I shake my head. "No idea."

"You're not going to ignore this, are you? The person knows your name. Could have something to do with your stories."

"I don't know." I shake my head, staring at the message. "This could be a prank. Or worse, some creepy serial killer."

Maxine snorts, covering her mouth to muffle her laughter. "Highly unlikely. Serial killers don't usually give advance notice. And besides, it's at the top of the Eiffel Tower. Pretty public place."

I roll my eyes but can't help the flicker of intrigue tugging at my curiosity.

I've been waiting to go up the Eiffel Tower ever since I arrived in Paris; I just never imagined it would be for a cryptic meeting with a faceless stranger.

"Maybe I'll go," I say, almost to myself. "And I could always leave if anything feels off. Besides, you're right. It's public."

"Exactly! And if you change your mind, just text me. I'll be there in a heartbeat," she says.

All through class I think about the message. The only person I know is hiding behind anything is Leo Montclair. But he's left Paris. Leif said so.

Who else could be hiding something from me?

LATER THAT EVENING, I FIND MYSELF WALKING towards the Eiffel Tower. The night air is cool and crisp, swirling around me as I get closer to the towering iron structure, alight with a soft, golden glow. The lines of tourists seem endless, stretching toward the elevators like an assembly line.

Standing at the base, I feel small, as if I'm at the feet of a giant. The tower reaches up into the night, its lights reflecting on the Seine. I close my eyes for a moment and remember another night, months ago, standing under these same lights with Leo by my side. We had watched the tower light up from his apartment, sharing wine and pastries, with Paris stretched out below us like a dream.

"Have you ever been to the top?" he had asked, his eyes twinkling as we looked out across the skyline.

I had shaken my head, biting my lip. *"It's on my list, but . . . not yet."*

"I promise, next time," he'd whispered. His hand had brushed mine, warm and solid. I could still feel the electricity in that touch, the unspoken promise.

Back in the present, the memory brings a bittersweet smile to my lips. The promise of a next time had been so casual, like we'd have all the time in the world. But that "next time" never came.

The elevator doors slide open, and I hand over my ticket, stepping inside with a slight tremble of anticipation. I've never been this high in the city. As we ascend, the lights of Paris start to spread out below me, sparkling like stars against the inky darkness. The view is breathtaking, but it's also a stark reminder of just how alone I am here.

At the top, a breeze sweeps across the open platform. I pull my scarf tighter around my shoulders, glancing around for anyone who looks like they might be waiting for me. I feel both excited and foolish, hoping this isn't some elaborate hoax.

Chapter Fifty-Eight

LEO

As soon as the plane touches down at Orly, I turn my phone back on, and the first thing I see is a notification from Daisy's social media account. She's posted a new message: *Meeting someone at the Eiffel Tower tonight at 10 pm. The mystery awaits.*

My pulse kicks up instantly. I check the time—it's already 9:40. "I need a car," I say to my assistant, practically shouting as I grab my bag and push through the cabin door.

A car is waiting on the tarmac, but Paris traffic is merciless this late at night, and it's barely moving as we approach the city center. I check my watch again—10:02. I can't let this chance slip away. "Stop here," I tell the driver. "I'll go on foot."

The driver tries to protest, but I'm already out, sprinting down the cobbled street and dodging late-night pedestrians.

My mind races as fast as my feet—is she meeting someone, who could it be? Has she found someone else? My heart aches at the thought. But right now, I don't care. I just need to see her, even if it's only to say goodbye.

Finally, the towering silhouette of the Eiffel Tower looms above, illuminated against the dark sky. I push past the crowd at the entrance, flashing my diplomatic passport to security.

"Right this way, Your Highness," a burly blue-suited man says. He directs me to the entrance of a side elevator, where I see my brother standing.

He thrusts an armful of pink daisies into my arms, "Go, she's been up there a while already."

"Leif? Was it you?"

He nods.

"You are the mystery person she's meeting up there?"

Leif holds open his phone. "Me, Father, and this guy."

James's face pops up on the phone screen. "Dude, you're wasting time talking to us. Being your indecisive Hamlet-self again. Move your ass."

Before I can tell James to shut up, Leif plays defense.

He frowns. "You can't speak to the future King of Arandel that way."

James snorts loudly. "I can because I'm going to be crowned King at the next Reed Dance. Guys, you need to bow please."

"Okay, where is the damn elevator?" I say hurriedly as I tap on the metal structure in front of me. The blue-suited man apologizes. "It's on its way, Your Highness."

I turn to Leif. "Did you say Father was in on this mystery rendezvous?"

He smiles. "It was his idea. He directed the whole thing from Arandel. I sent him Daisy's website. And he read about her Anthology of Love Lock stories raising money for rural villages in Senegal. He's very impressed. His exact words were, 'Why has Leo been hiding this beautiful gem?'"

"Yeah, why?" I ask, disgusted with myself but thankful to Leif and Father.

The elevator doors slide open finally, and I step in, clutching the daisies. "Thanks for the flowers, Leif."

He nods. "Don't mess up. Do you even know how to grovel?"

"Do you?" I snap back.

"Hurry up," I hear him shout as the bell pings on the elevator before the doors close.

"Don't lose our future Queen." Leif is grinning in a way I've not seen in a long time.

"Thanks, dude."

His eyes shine. "I've been wondering if you'd ever call me that. Or if that was a term of endearment only for your best friend."

"It's only for me," James shouts on the phone. I leave Leif and James to argue about who gets called what as the doors finally slide closed.

I tap my hand nervously on the metal rail inside the cavernous service elevator. Apparently, the VIP one was being used by a hip-hop mogul vacationing in Paris.

The entire way up, I pace inside the vast space meant for loading and unloading food and crafts for the restaurants and souvenir shops in the Tower.

Do I even know how to grovel?" I ask myself in the mirrored walls. I swipe my hair back and straighten my suit, which is disheveled after my jog through the cold streets. At least I'm not sweaty.

After what seems like a march across Mongolia, the elevator doors open with a soft ding, and I step onto the observation deck, scanning for any sign of her.

It's almost 11 pm. A whole hour has passed since she was supposed to meet the mystery person. I'm terrified she might have already left.

I walk around the observation deck.

Where could she be? Meanwhile, at the side of my eye, I see the dazzling display of Paris lights below.

Where is the woman who rivals these lights?

Kingdom of Arandel

Chapter Fifty-Nine

DAISY

I should have known this was some kind of scheme. And I've fallen for it.

Because I want to live the fairy tale so badly. I want to be the girl who meets the love of her life at the top of an iconic building, amidst lights and the rush of love . . . also known as adrenaline. Isn't that all love really is? A chemical reaction to a vision that excites you.

For me, the vision is a tall, blond guy with icy blue eyes whose dazzling smile knocks me off my feet.

Part of me deep down, okay, maybe not so deep, very much on the surface—hoped my mystery messenger would lead me to Leo.

I thought I could have a rendezvous at the top of the Eiffel Tower the way Meg Ryan in *Sleepless in Seattle* and Mindy Lahiri on *The Mindy Project* did on top of the Empire State Building.

If it wasn't for the fact that Mindy waited a very long time at the top of the Empire State Building for Danny Castellano to show up, I'd have gone back down in the elevator already. I'd have bought a hot chocolate at one of the food trucks at the base of the

Tower and drank it while watching the lights twinkle. I'd have been okay.

But no, thanks to Mindy's tenacity, I feel as if I must stay here, in the cold, holding on to my belief of true love, and my desire for The One. I want my fairy tale, too.

I stroll around the perimeter of the platform, admiring the dazzling lights below. The whole of Paris is at my feet. The bridges, the river, the cafés and bookstores, the boulevards, the dreams and hopes and desires of thousands of people who come to Paris like me, to find themselves amongst the treasures of art and light.

It doesn't get better than this.

My inner voice whispers, "You are your own fairy tale." Because what is a fairy tale but a journey to be whole? The princess starts off with pieces of herself missing. In *Cinderella*. In *Snow White*. In *Beauty & the Beast*. The girl has lost her mother, like me.

Maybe when a girl loses her mother, she loses an essential part of herself. And the story of making yourself whole is your fairy tale: Prince or no prince.

Although a prince would be excellent, too.

I stare at the lights and give my mother in heaven a smile. I'm closer to her up here than I've ever been. In body and spirit.

"Hey, Mom, I miss you," I whisper to the cold night air.

A sudden warmth envelops me like a warm hug.

I know I'm being fanciful, but it feels as if my mother is standing here next to me. I am not alone. No matter who walks, or doesn't walk, through that door.

The wind picks up, blowing my curls into my eyes.

I wrap my scarf around and around my face like a mummy.

Whoever this mystery person is, they better show up. I'm leaving at 11 pm when the sparkly lights dance up and down the Tower again.

I'm leaving when the lights stop blinking.

Chapter Sixty

LEO

There she is, standing at the edge, looking out over Paris like she's part of it, her silhouette blending with the lights shimmering across the city.

My Daisy. My beautiful, sweet Daisy.

I think my heart stops. Literally. Although my hand holding the daisies is shaking so much I have to put them down on the landing.

She turns, as if sensing me, and our eyes lock. She's wrapped up so tightly in a scarf that I can barely see her face, but it's her—my one and only.

"Daisy," I breathe. My voice catches. "Daisy," I say again, more firmly.

She unwraps the scarf slowly, revealing her cold red cheeks and her rosebud mouth. I want to dash over to her and grab her in my arms. But I restrain myself.

This is the most important moment of my life so far, and I can't mess it up.

Her hand goes to her throat. For a long, breathless moment, neither of us moves.

"Leo?" Her voice is soft, stunned.

Then, she bursts into tears.

I don't hold back any longer. I race to her and catch her as she sinks into my arms.

Her hands are icicles. "You're so cold, my love." I rub her hands and stick them in my pockets. "Where are your gloves?"

She shakes her head. "I didn't know I'd be up here so long."

"I'm sorry, baby. I'm so so sorry. For everything. But firstly, I'm sorry that I'm late."

She's staring at me as if I'm not real. I think I'm looking at her the same way.

Then, I'm crying too. Tears course down our cheeks and mingle together into fragments of ice.

"I missed you, Leo. I am so mad at you for leaving me."

I shake my head. "I'm more angry at myself than anyone can be. Baby, I hope you'll let me show you how sorry I am."

A slight smile tugs at her lips as she stands up fully out of my arms.

Already, I feel bereft.

"Your closeness is what I need to feel right. I hope you will forgive me, Daisy."

She looks down, letting the words sink in, then turns back to me. Her eyes are steady, searching mine, and it feels like everything we've been holding back is right here between us. It never went away.

My pulse pounds, and without a word, I reach for her face, holding it like I've always meant to. Her fingers lace with mine, grounding me in this moment.

She gives a small smile, like she can't quite believe I'm real. "You've been with me," she says softly. "Every day. I don't think I could have forgotten you if I tried."

Her words linger, and I pull her closer, my arms wrapping around her like she belongs there. Our faces are close, and I see every quiet moment we've shared, every unspoken promise, all in her eyes.

Then, slowly, I lean in, our lips meeting with a tenderness that feels both familiar and new, like something we've both been waiting for.

Around us, the lights of the Eiffel Tower begin to sparkle, casting Paris in gold and silver. And in that moment, nothing else matters—just her, just us, finally where we're meant to be.

Chapter Sixty-One

DAISY

As Leo and I step into the elevator, I can't help but laugh, a mix of nerves and exhilaration bubbling up inside. We're so close, hands clasped tightly, and he keeps drawing me into kisses between our words.

Every time our lips meet, my mind goes blank except for one resounding thought: this is real.

When we reach the bottom, his hand never leaves mine, guiding me to a sleek black limo waiting by the curb.

Leo opens the door with a small, playful bow, and I slide in, unable to contain my smile.

"This is yours?" I ask, surprised such a luxurious car is hanging around waiting for him.

"And yours," he says.

I scoot close to him, my head resting on his shoulder as he wraps both arms around me. It feels like coming home.

"Where to, my princess?" he asks softly, his breath warm against my temple.

I glance up, my face still glowing from our kisses. "Let's drive around Paris," I whisper, kissing his cheek. "Let's see everything—together."

He chuckles, running his hand through my hair. "I'll take you anywhere you want. By the way, my love, I have something to tell you."

I wave a hand. "Nothing matters now."

"Okay," he says. "I just thought you should know."

I roll my eyes. "I don't care what it is . . . I love you . . . you love me . . . nothing else matters."

"Fine," he says with a smile.

At that moment the driver turns to us, "Where to Your Highness?"

Leo looks at me, "Anywhere you said, right?"

But my eyes are glued on the driver and then back to Leo.

"What did you call him?" I sound rude as heck, but the driver smiles.

It's Leo who speaks. "Your Royal Highness, Crown Prince of Arandel, at your service, Miss."

My mouth falls so far open that I must be drooling on the dark luxury seats.

I am not a person who curses ever, but a word comes out of my mouth I'd never say.

"Oh, duck!"

Leo laughs. "As you were saying, nothing matters. Not even that I am a Prince, right?"

I smack him on his shoulder. "Yes, that matters, Leo. What the duck!"

The drive winds us all around Paris. For most of the drive, we're kissing so much we miss the big sites. The rest of the drive is me asking a million questions about what this means.

As we drive past the gleaming pyramid of the Louvre, Leo says, "One of the perks of being a future king is that we can get into most places after hours. In case you want to see the Mona Lisa up close."

My stomach flips. A future king. "How long do we have together, Leo?" I ask, heart pounding. "When do you have to leave again?"

He gently tilts my chin so I'm looking straight into his eyes, full of warmth and resolve. "Daisy," he murmurs, brushing a stray curl behind my ear, "I'm not leaving you. I'm done with running, with hiding. I want you to meet my family, my mother and father. This weekend, if you'll come with me to Arandel."

I blink, surprised. His parents? "Oh, Leo. But . . . this weekend I promised Maxine we'd go to Provence together."

He laughs. "Bring her along! I'll arrange everything." His blue eyes sparkle with the thrill of it. "Anyone you want can come."

"Really?" I grin, my mind racing. "What about my sister Emerald?"

Leo raises an eyebrow, laughing. "Emerald? Don't you two argue all the time?"

"Maybe," I say with a shy smile. "But this is something she should see for herself. And honestly, I'd love for you to meet her."

He nods, pulling me close again. "Then let's do it. Call her."

I pull out my phone, dialing Emerald, and within moments, her voice is in my ear, a blend of worry and excitement. "Daisy? Are you okay? I saw that cryptic post about meeting a stranger at the Eiffel Tower! Are you safe?"

I can't help but laugh, the joy spilling out. "Guess what, sis? I got my fairy tale. I wanted you to be the first to know."

There's silence on the other end, then the loudest whoop I've ever heard. I have to hold the phone away, my smile spreading wider with each second. I bite my lip, practically giddy.

Emerald's voice softens, full of happiness and pride. "I love you, sis."

"I love you, too, sis."

Then I turn to Leo. "And you, my King, I am crazy about you."

Chapter Sixty-Two

DAISY

My first glimpse of Arandel is enough to take my breath away.

It's not just the rugged mountains that tower over the land, or the delicious scented trees lining the long driveway; it's the pride on Leo's face as he points out the fields and rivers, the village with its festive Christmas tree in the center, as tall as the sky and lit up as if by fairies flitting and swooping around it.

He grins at me, "I tried to recreate the blinking lights of the Eiffel Tower that flash every hour."

"This is better than the Tower. It goes on forever."

"Forever," he says, rubbing my wrist encircled by a simple silver bracelet with the word "*Forever*" engraved in the same script as the love lock.

It's his first gift to me and it's everything.

My nerves at meeting the King and Queen disappeared as soon as I saw their warm smiles of welcome. I'm not sure if the smiles were their way of being polite or if they were sincere, but I'll take it.

I did a perfect curtesy before them just like I'd practiced half my life in front of my bedroom's large pink mirror.

I had to bite my lip to stop giggling at the memory of curtseying before my dolls back home.

The Christmas Ball is on the eighth day before Christmas, a holiday in Arandel.

I couldn't wait to wear my gorgeous ball gown. When Lulu heard I would be attending the Ball at Arandel and that Leo was the Crown Prince, she said she was making my dress, whether I liked it or not.

"Of course, I *love* it," I'd said.

Lulu had been excited that one of her designs would be worn to meet royalty. She was calling her new designs, *Lulu's Princess Line*.

"I'm not a princess, Lulu," I'd said.

"Yet," she retorted, holding the gossamer fabric up to my body and wrapping it around me.

The completed gown should be in a museum. It is that spectacular. The blush-colored fabric is as light as butterfly wings. The fabric drapes softly over my shoulders, and the silky dress ripples and flows like water when I walk.

Leo stares at me in stunned silence as I glide down the castle stairs.

I've seriously been practicing for this moment in my head forever.

To see a look of pure adoration on a man's face looking up at me as I enter a room makes my heart skip a million beats.

Happiness pours out of me in waves.

I am the Eiffel Tower. I am the Empire State Building. I am the Taj Mahal, and everything that is special and beautiful.

I, Daisy Walker, have gotten my fairy tale.

THE HALL GLOWS IN SOFT LIGHTS, CASTING A GOLDEN warmth over everyone. The music is lively, filling the air with holiday spirit as friends and family mingle, laugh, and dance.

Leo squeezes my hand, his eyes shining, and I can't believe we're here, together, surrounded by everyone we love.

Although not everyone loves me! I've noticed a few young women who expected to meet Leo as an eligible future King are now eyeing me with distaste.

Leo also notices, pushing Leif to meet the invited guests from near and far.

"Your future bride is most likely here tonight," Leo says to Leif, who grins and says, "Maybe, brother. But I don't need to get married."

James thanks me for finally giving Crown Prince Leo a second chance. "I'd never have heard the end of this if you hadn't."

I bow my head. "Thank you, Prince James."

Maxine comes bouncing up for an introduction. When I tell her he's a Prince of the Zulu Nation, Maxine swoons.

She returns to my side after she recovers from Prince James' charms and killer smile.

"So, are you two finally going to make it official?" Maxine gives Leo and me a shy grin. "You're the only ones who haven't toasted each other!"

I laugh, glancing at Leo, who raises a brow in amusement.

"Official? We're practically Paris's worst-kept secret," he says, chuckling. "But . . . if it's a toast you want . . . ."

Before he can finish, Lulu whirls over, a drink in hand, looking between us. "You two, seriously. Toast each other right now, or Maxine and I will make up some absurd speech for you."

Leo gives me a wink, lifting his glass. "Alright, alright," he says, clearing his throat dramatically. "To Daisy . . . who has somehow put up with me this long and still has the patience to be here tonight."

Everyone laughs, and I roll my eyes, nudging him. "To Leo, who somehow managed to find his way back to me even when I didn't know how much I needed him."

There's a round of cheers, and then Emerald, who arrived last night, appears beside me, smiling. "Daisy, this is amazing," she says, giving me a quick hug. "I never thought I'd see you looking so . . . radiant. What's your secret?"

"Could it be Paris?" I tease, and we both laugh. "Or maybe it's just having all of you here." I glance over at Leo, who's now deep in conversation with Leif, both of them laughing and sharing some brotherly moment I don't quite catch.

Emerald and I exchange glances, smiling. "They are alike," she says, shaking her head. "Even though they think they're not. Kind of like us."

"Yes, exactly."

Leif catches Emerald's eye, tipping his glass with a grin. "Careful there," he says, overhearing us. "I've always been the mature one."

Maxine snorts, coming up behind him. "Sure, Leif. The only thing you've mastered is how to dance without spilling your drink."

We all laugh as Leif strikes an exaggerated pose, his glass held high, then spins Emerald onto the dance floor, drawing applause from the guests around us.

As the music slows, Leo pulls me back into his arms. "Think

they'll ever stop teasing us?" he murmurs, his voice low, just for me.

"Not a chance," I reply, laughing as Maxine and Lulu join hands and twirl each other across the floor, leaving a path of laughter and joy behind them.

From across the room, Leif shouts, "Alright, alright—if anyone deserves the spotlight, it's the two of you. A final toast to Leo and Daisy!"

Leo says he can't believe the change in Leif. James agrees. "It's as if he was waiting on something and finally got it."

"Waiting to be seen and acknowledged," Leo says. "Like everyone."

The guests cheer, lifting their glasses, and I feel a warmth spread through me, knowing that this, right here, is the happiest I've ever been. Leo smiles down at me, his gaze steady and full of everything we've been through.

"Looks like they're making us the stars of the show," he whispers, pulling me closer.

I smile, holding him tight. "As long as it's with you, I wouldn't want it any other way."

I HOPE YOU ENJOYED ***PARIS FOREVER!***

Please consider leaving a review. Reviews help authors get noticed.

About the Author

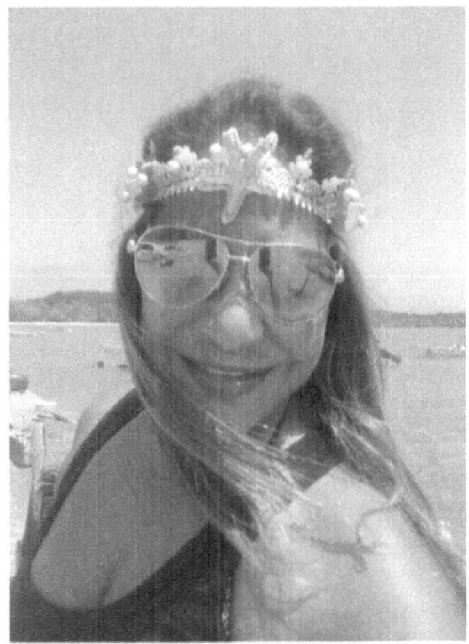

Lynn Joseph is from Trinidad & Tobago. When she's not writing her international romances, she can be found on a beach somewhere in the world. Or binge-watching *Hart of Dixie* and *The Vampire Diaries* over and over. Lynn lives in charming South Portland, Maine, and on the Caribbean Island of Tobago, where she's known as the Mermaid Queen. Join her on her journey of love, food, and romantic destinations (not necessarily in that order). www.lynnjosephbooks.com

Stay Connected

Sign up for Lynn's newsletter and receive a FREE ebook, *Princess Aboard.* Plus be in the know for all the behind the scenes goodies and more!

Sign Up Here —>
https://BookHip.com/NKSQGRS

Follow her on social media:

Facebook -http://facebook.com/lynnjosephauthor
Instagram - https://www.instagram.com/lynnjosephbooks/
Bookbub - https://bit.ly/3Phcsuu
Amazon - https://amzn.to/3VTd8Kb
Goodreads -https://bit.ly/4gUtZo4

Lynn loves to hear from her readers and invites them to email her, anytime at lynn@lynnjosephbooks.com

www.lynnjosephbooks.com

Also by Lynn Joseph

The Walker Sisters Forever Series

(Sweet Romance)

Gelato Forever

Olives Forever

Sangria Forever

Paris Forever

Christmas Forever

Cocoa Reef Resort Series

(Steamy Romance)

Lime to My Coconut

Rum to the Reggae

Spice for My Santa

Princess Abroad

(Read for FREE! —> https://BookHip.com/NKSQGRS)

www.ingramcontent.com/pod-product-compliance
Lightning Source LLC
Chambersburg PA
CBHW032235310726
48973CB00008B/2146

9798988048695